TABLE OF CONTENTS

Rewind - A Collection

Acknowledgements	VII
Foreword from As I Am	1
Before You Judge by Roisín Coyne	2
Bev & The Egg timer by Grainne Toher	3
Greenhills by Kay Forristal	11
A Small Decent Thing by Martin Hand	17
In Loving Memory by Emma Davis	26
Ghost by Leigh Kenny	28
The Loop by D.C. Spuera	31
My First Car by Betty O'Mahony	41
My Grandfather by John Joe McGinley	44
Lucky Lucas by David Bowmore	46
The Importance Of The Consistent by Fiona Gill	50
Chestnut Heaven by Eoin Brady	53

Summer Fair by Catherine Kullmann 59

Spare Parts by Anne McDonald 64

An Open Wound by Eamon Ó Cléirigh 67

Eileen by Mary Minnock 72

The Sun is Not At The Table
by Eileen Moynihan 78

Memories by Bernadette O'Reilly 83

Heartbreak Ridge by Mary M. Trant 84

Bog Trippin' by Alex Secam 88

Zoe's Birthday Party By Roisín Coyne 97

The Light Between Us
by Joanne Ryan Curran 99

Watching by Yvonne Brewer 105

Galway by Val Robus 108

Sky Words by Kathryn Crowley 111

Granted by Eamon O'Leary 113

Grandfather's Clock by Niall O'Connor 123

Leaving Home by Tom Moloney 125

O'Malley's Ghost by Robert McDermott 132
The Happiness Clinic by Camilla Galbiati 142
The Deepness of the Brave by Orla McConnon Bakerberg 152
Leading Lady by Mary Egan Campbell 155
The Red Velvet Box by Mary T. Bradford 161
Missing Pieces by Denis Ahern 169
Erase & Rewind by Claire O'Connor 172
Nothing Compares With You by Kerry Manning 183
Silent Wounds by Theresa Hiney Tinggal 186
Remembering Ophelia by Carolann Copland 189
Fallow Ground by Martin Daly 199
Doubt by Sandra Matthews 210
End of The Road by Aislín O'Neill 212
That Year by Helen O'Sullivan 222
False memories by Rory Dwayne 231
The Stations by Mary Heeran White 233

Fragments of My Mother by T.O. Munro 241
A Lasting Impression by Ethel Corduff 251

Get to Know The Author - Bios 254
About Indie Authors Ireland 263

Acknowledgements

Thanks to each and everyone of you who submitted to this wonderful collection! Thanks to all who took the time to come together to collect ideas, brainstorm and make decisions. Special thanks to everyone who volunteered to proofread and did so with the utmost professionalism and speed.

A hat tip and a group hug to the anthology team for their support and hard work. For the hours of work whether it was editing, rescuing lost files, or the good humour and stubborn enthusiasm.

A special mention for volunteering professional services

Editor **Eamon Ó Cléirigh**

of Clearview Fiction https://clearviewfictionediting.com/

Book Designer Amanda Horan

of Let's Get Booked https://www.letsgetbooked.com/

Author Emma Davis https://fairyfortpublications.bigcartel.com/

Together we've managed to make a great collection for a worthy cause. Kudos to all!

Foreword from As I Am

www.asiam.ie

In the words of Oscar Wilde, "memories are the diary that we all carry with us". They can evoke powerful emotion personally, transporting us to places and experiences that once were. They can also play an important collective role in our society – forging our shared experience, identity, and culture. At our best, communities engage constructively and truthfully with memories of the past in order to acknowledge and learn from historic wrongs.

It is often said that "there is no point looking back", and yet, if we fail to look back, we fail to reflect, and we risk never moving forward at all. AsIAm is Ireland's Autism Charity, and our vision is to bring about a society in Ireland in which every Autistic person is accepted as they are – equal, valued, and respected. In looking forward and working towards this vision, it is critical we remember the journey that countless Autistic people, and our community as a whole, have taken so far, and the pervasive barriers which have too often stood in our way.

We remember an Ireland of institutions and stigma. An Ireland which underdiagnosed and failed to educate Autistic people. We remember a time where we heard about Autism but never from Autistic people. In many ways, the Ireland of 2025 is foreign to that of 2015 or 2005 or 1995 when it comes to awareness and knowledge of Autism in Ireland. Yet awareness does not mean acceptance, and knowledge does not mean action. Often, stigmatising views on Autism sit just below the surface. Autistic people and parents still must fight for basic supports in both the classroom and the community, which at times can create a sense of de ja vu – as problems and failures are repeated again and again by State actors.

Most recently, we have seen growing misinformation about Autism in the public square, often driven by those with no lived experience. All of this tells me that to move forward we must keep our memories firmly to the fore and alive in our discourse.

This book is a powerful example of keeping memory alive and engaging with it, in its broadest form and across a wide range of perspectives and expressions. That the authors so generously gave of their time and talent to bring together this publication, in support of our charity, means a great deal. This publication will not only raise much-needed funds in support of our work but also provides another opportunity for AsIAm to reach more people – be they those who may benefit from our support, or those who need to hear that simple message that every Autistic person must have the same chance to live, work, and play in their community.

I am particularly delighted that Roisín Coyne has contributed her work to this volume – an important example of Autistic voice and one of the most talented young creatives in our community.

I hope all who read "Rewind" will have time and space to unwind as you embark on a trip down memory lane.

Adam Harris

Founder and CEO of As I Am

Before You Judge

A message from Roisín Coyne

Before you judge someone, you should get to know their story first.

You will never know who you are speaking to unless you walk with them, instead of away from them.

A story will not be told by guesswork, or assumptions you hear about them.

Ask them about themselves, don't join the shadows that may follow them around.

Be the light that they may need.

Bev & The Egg Timer

Grainne Toher

The 'Ashanti' retreat centre stood on its own plot of land against the backdrop of the Atlantic's crashing waves. It was a converted old two-storey farmhouse with outhouses, which would, in the fullness of time, become sheds, a sauna, and holistic therapy rooms.

"Can I not get a bigger business loan than fifty thousand?" the owner of Ashanti, Beverly O'Callaghan, had asked Paddy O'Driscoll, manager of the local bank. "Sure, won't I be bringing tourists and everything into the area, boosting local business?"

"Ask me again in a year,' Paddy replied. "If they a really cleaning up like you say, it shouldn't be an issue."

Bev was more of a dreamer than a businessperson. She had inherited the house from a distant aunt and wanted to make this work.

"I've burned through thirty thousand already on the construction work alone!" she'd complained to her mother.

Her mother, Margaret, remained tight-lipped, having sunk many euros into her daughter's hare brained schemes over the years, while living frugally herself as a result.

"I *can't* get cheap stuff," Bev whined to her boyfriend Jim. "It is meant to be an exclusive boutique experience after all."

"That rules out Jysk and IKEA so," Jim said, smiling as he headed for the golf course. He had already helped out with the heavy lifting and the painting and would not be derailed this time from the eighteen holes he'd booked.

Bev scoured the internet for the best furniture, bedding, crockery, and soft furnishings. The last twenty thousand of her bank loan wasn't long disappearing but she told herself she would somehow manage everything else.

Margaret and Bev set to work assembling the furniture, making up the bedrooms, and positioning the fixtures and fittings about in a tasteful way. The boutique retreat experience was coming together. The two women hugged each other as they surveyed their handy work. Harvey Norman couches were placed in the breakout areas. Emma beds were in every bedroom, dressed in Arnotts' bedding, and yoga-themed ornaments and pictures filled the blank spaces. Since the Ashanti website launched with its beautiful imagery, their treat bookings had been flying in. The first busload would arrive that coming Friday. An anxious Bev could not believe the day was almost here.

Helena Kelly, the yoga teacher, arrived down from Dublin on the Thursday night, winding her way through the country roads to Ashanti, having stopped off in Ennis for her dinner. Next day, she got up early, opened the fridge in the centre's kitchen, and saw a bottle of orange juice and a litre of oat milk. It was otherwise bare.

She scratched her head and made her way to the yoga studio, where she met Bev. The large studio's windows looked out onto the wild Atlantic.

"Can you not put the heat on?" she asked.

"Oh, sure the sun will warm the room in a few minutes, "Bev said. "Do you want a blanket for now?"

Helena shivered. "Go on, I will."

The pair enjoyed a lovely stretch, followed by a relaxation session. Admittedly, the weather was mild for April, and the sun did shine. If these conditions kept up, they might even get to do a bit of practice on the beach. Helena's students were following her down by minibus from Dublin today. They had saved for months, and this was a big treat for them. Helena's mother, Eithne, herself a fit pensioner, would be arriving at lunchtime.

"Let's go out for breakfast," Bev said after the stretch.

Helena agreed, although she had not budgeted for breakfast.

"Be nice to have a look around," she said as they got into her car.

They found a rustic little café in Fanore and ordered two big breakfasts. Bev had a second round of toast and another pot of tea. As the waitress brought the bill, Bev had a sudden and urgent need for the bathroom. Helena was irked but paid the bill, reasoning that at least she could expense it. Bev gushed at the waitress about the food and the service, name-dropping Ashanti at every opportunity to all who could hear and promised to bring all her guests there.

"Do you mind if we stop at Lidl?" she asked a stony-faced Helena.

"Sure," Helena said, sighing through gritted teeth, telling herself that she liked to load up, anyway, on healthy snacks to maintain her blood-sugar levels when she was away from her own kitchen.

Bev popped some oats, fruit, eggs, and yoghurt into a basket. "My mother makes the most delicious soda bread."

She would want to, thought Helena. It wouldn't do to let her menopausal yoga gang coming from Dublin get hangry.

"Oh no, I think I left my wallet back at the centre, "Bev cried. 'Do you mind covering it and I'll sort you out later?' Bev had no intention of it. Let Helena expense it, sure she had plenty of money.

Helena did so, but grudgingly.

Her mood lifted later as her arriving yoginis looked around, impressed with the plush surroundings.

"Bags the green room with the sea view," said Josie, a Dublin yogi in her late fifties from the inner city.

"I'm bunking in with you," Marie said. She was along-term student of Helena's, who lived a few doors down from Josie.

The centre was soon full of the banter and roars of inner-city midlife mams in need of a break from family life. Helena and her mam were in one of the quiet rooms at the back of the house, delighted to have time to catch up together – a rare treat.

After an evening stretch and a spot of seated breathwork in the studio to centre the guests, a catered vegetarian curry arrived. It was a bit lukewarm but hunger was a good sauce and it soon pacified the frowns and murmurs of the guests.

Fruit and herbal teas awaited the waking guests next morning, after which they rolled out yoga mats in the studio and enjoyed a decent workout followed by a long relaxation session. When class was over, the hungry yogis descended on the kitchen, a gorgeous smell of fresh coffee hitting their nostrils. Each one grabbed a spot at the expensive Harvey Norman tile-topped table.

Ten tiny glass jars with a spoonful of porridge oats, a spoonful of natural yoghurt, and a solitary blueberry sat on the countertop. A bowl of boiled eggs beside the jars was dwarfed by big plates of buttered homemade soda bread.

"Here, can we take two eggs?" a ravenous Josie asked.

"There's one for everyone in the audience," Bev said, smiling to an unimpressed crowd surveying the tiny meal.

Eithne took her breakfast to the table and ran to her bedroom to grab her carefully prepared tablet collection. Helena served herself. Just as she turned towards the table, she spotted a greedy Bev whipping the boiled egg off poor Eithne's plate. Enough was enough.

"Oi, you, put that back," she roared. "And I want a word, outside."

Knowing Helena to be slow to anger unless she had good reason, her students were confident she would soon sort it out. They giggled as they looked out the window at the roars, pointed fingers, red faces, and pleas going on.

Josie laughed. "I'm having her egg."

"Well then, I'll take her porridge," Eithne exclaimed.

Next thing, Bev jumped into her car, screeched off, and powered down the road.

"I tell ya," Marie said as a red-faced Helena came back in gasping for coffee, "if that Bev one is not on her way to a supermarket to fill up this kitchen, she'd be better off not coming back at all with us lot here."

Helena grinned. "I wonder who she's going to shaft now to feed us."

A mile down the road, Bev pulled in, still shaking after the dressing down from Helena. With clouds darkening and raindrops hitting the dashboard, she lifted out her phone. As she thumbed through the contacts, she ruled out her two sisters, who were not speaking to her at the minute for a variety of reasons she didn't want to think about. She couldn't bother Jim or her mam again so soon, as she would probably need them for something else before long. And she had long since burned bridges with close friends, so they would hardly pick up.

She started up the engine again and drove on. Further down the road, she came upon a freshly painted sign chained high on a post outside a big farmhouse: 'Fresh Hen Eggs'. It must be new, as she hadn't spotted it before. Wondering if they might give her a bit of food on tick, she made her way around the piles of cow dung and puddles towards the back door. It was open and there seemed to be no one around.

"Could I be cheeky enough to help myself?" she asked herself as she sought out the hen house. "Desperate times and desperate measures, and all that."

As she opened the door to the clucking sounds, a hen strode out and ran past her.

"Oi, Oi," came an angry voice. A young blond farmer hopped over the wall in wellingtons and ran to rescue the hen before it reached the road. "Oi!" he shouted again.

It was Bev's second 'Oi' of the morning and, unable to stop herself, she burst into tears.

"Ah now, sure there's no need to be crying. What's the matter with you?"

Bev couldn't miss how handsome the farmer was. She sobbed as she looked up at him through wet eyelashes, and described how desperate she felt, telling him how her dream Ashanti was all about to come crashing down before it even began.

The farmer regarded her running nose, red face, and wild brown hair, and considered her quite pretty for a thief. "What's your name, anyway?"

"Bev." She sniffed as the tears welled up again.

"Well, Bev, my name is Mike, and I'll tell you what –we have plenty of homegrown food here, not just hen eggs. If I give you a bag of our own spuds, cabbages, eggs, goats' milk and cheese, butter, and carrots, will you let me sit in on a couple of your classes? I've always wanted to try yoga, and farm life can be stressful, so maybe a bit of mindfulness might help."

Bev couldn't believe her luck. "I'll tell you what, Mike, if we can come to some sort of arrangement around food, you and all your family will have free yoga and meditation at Ashanti for life. How does that sound?"

Mike smiled. "I think we can chat a bit more about that. Why don't you come in for a quick coffee?"

Bev dried her eyes and followed him towards the backdoor of his farmhouse. Putting her wet tissue into her coat pocket, she looked up at the sky and noticed that the rain had stopped, and the sun was coming out again.

Greenhills

Kay Forristal

My mother, Maisie Ryan, was the only member of her family to marry and bear children, and simply loved her role as wife, mother, and housekeeper. She slipped as neatly into family life as a foot into a slipper, and in manner, she was one of the gentlest people you could meet. As the youngest of a family of ten children, I spent the majority of my time with her. She had an interesting way of telling a story and revealing interesting information that I could always grasp and retain. At night, when the house was quiet, Mam sat with a copy book writing down her thoughts and writing poetry. I would stand behind her, combing her hair and asking countless questions, while Dad sat at the other end of the table, a row of tacks between his lips, mending our shoes with a hammer and last. Mam made up stories to keep me entertained, and when I was a little older, she read me Aesop's fables and later again the classics, including Jane Eyre and other Brontë novels.

My mother's character was, as with all of us, formed by her early life. She came from Greenhills, Moneygall in County Offaly. Her parents took the decision to emigrate to America when she was seven years old. Their passage was booked, and she remembered her father packing all their china, oil lamps, and linen into large tea chests for the journey, but before they were set to depart, her mother contracted tuberculosis. All her life, she remembered how on her First Holy Communion Day, when she returned home to tell her mother all about the ceremonies, she was met with the news that her mother had died. It affected her deeply for the rest of her life.

Each year, my mother brought me to visit 'Greenhills', her childhood home in Moneygall. I loved all the farm activity, especially watching the hens clucking around the yard. All the cows on the farm had names, as had all the cats. There was a large orchard stood at one side of the house, and green fields dotted with haycocks stretched out, so that I could play wherever I liked. A small back porch led into the kitchen, with its large dresser displaying glass and china, and also oil lamps and ornaments. My godmother, Aunt Kathleen, was kind and generous, if a little fussy. If I picked something up, I had to put it down inexactly the same place.

The kitchen was always hot because she never let the range out, even on a summer's day. She and her brothers, John and Jimmy, were set in their ways and not used to having children moving around to disturb them. Grace was always said before and after meals. Aunt Kathleen stressed the importance of manners, saying that they brought sweetness to everything. She had a lovely little cocker spaniel named Goldie, and she lavished attention on him as if he were a baby. He even had a bib and his own silver bowl.

When I look back, I think Aunt Kathleen envied my mother and the love she shared with my dad. She once asked Mam what the secret of a happy marriage was. Mam thought for a while,

"The success of any partnership is the accumulation of kind thoughts and the appreciation shown to one another," she said.

"And the demise of a relationship?"

"The death of a relationship comes through the accumulation of slights and the lack of attention that invariably led to taking another person for granted."

When I was older, Aunt Kathleen worked as matron of Saint Brigid's hospital in Carrick-on-Suir, County Tipperary. When she came home from work, she prepared supper and did her chores. Then she fetched her medical bag and brought me along to visit elderly people in the village. Here I saw the fullness of her kindness and generosity. One elderly woman she visited lived alone and was very lonely. Aunt Kathleen greeted her with a kiss, made her something to eat, and then she washed her feet in a basin of soapy water, gently removed the hard skin from her tired feet and massaged her legs. All the time, she chatted to the woman of times past and the people whom they had known and loved. She helped the woman put on her nightdress and saw her safely into bed before we left to visit the woman's brother.

I saw her make a poultice for a boil and place it on a man's neck and carefully dress his ulcerous legs. Elsewhere, I watched her clean festered wounds and bandage hurt limbs. Before leaving a house, she and the occupants would always share a prayer.

In Aunt Kathleen's youth, she had fostered a desire to be a nun but she felt a duty to care for her bachelor brothers. She genuinely cared for people, and this is how she fulfilled her vocation.

When Mam and I visited 'Greenhills', we slept in the sitting room. I liked it because it had a carpet, a fireplace, and lovely embossed wallpaper. A huge picture hung on one wall with fancy writing on it, decorated with a deep border of fine shells. My grandmother had made it. The room was well furnished and had a silver tea service on a silver tray, and rugs with country scene sprinted on them. During the night, Mam and I had long conversations, whispering in the darkness until sleep claimed us.

Every day we went for long walks, stopping along the road to pass the time of day with people she knew, and sometimes having a cup of tea with them. I had a favourite place that I never tired of hearing about and seeing. We crossed a stile and roamed through farmland until we came to the ruins of a rambling old house, standing on a hill. I was mesmerized when Mam told me stories of the people who had lived there, the grandeur of that stately home with its winding staircase and magnificent furnishings. My great-grandfather had been the head gardener of the estate. She had a wistful smile on her face when she remembered people coming in their horse-drawn carriages, driving through the gates, alighting at the mansion, and exiting through the other gate in a semi-circle. Pear trees stood at the back of the house, and she picked a golden delicious pear for me to eat as we walked around.

I saw a different side to my mother when she was in her original setting. This had been her home, and the people had been her people. Now they all looked so old, and she seemed sad, as if she didn't fit in and was looking for something that she had lost and could not find – maybe a part of herself.

She showed me the places where she had played as a youngster and told me she had been a fat child, and the other children had jeered her and called her "Fatty Arabuckle." I couldn't ever imagine my lovely petite mother being a fat child, but since she always told the truth, it must have been so.

Aunt Kathleen visited us in Listowel at least twice a year. Happily, my dad liked her, but her arrival meant that he was going to lose my mother for a week.

When I was twelve, Aunt Kathleen arrived with a caravan hitched to her car. That year we went to Wexford town. I had never stayed in a caravan before, and each day we drove to a different town and explored it. We brought a flask of tea and a picnic and sat on riverbanks and in sunny meadows to have our lunch, and in the evening, we went to a hotel for dinner. Sometimes, we went to a pub to hear music, and then back to the caravan to read or listen to the radio before turning in for the night in our miniature but comfortable beds. We were all good travellers and enjoyed this type of holiday immensely.

Aunt Kathleen took photographs everywhere we went. When we returned, we got a great welcome from dad. By the age of twelve, I was well-travelled due to the generosity of my aunt.

Sixty years later, in 2015, my partner, Chris, and I returned to Moneygall. I knew it would be a nostalgic journey, remembering my mother and all the Ryan family. I had a knot of excitement in my stomach as I searched frantically for the house or even a glimpse of the orchard wall but instead I saw The Barack Obama Plaza, named after US president Barack Obama, whose third great-grandfather lived in Moneygall and who emigrated to the US in 1850.

Overwhelmed by emotion, the tears came fast and furious. When the crying subsided, I realised that I had been locked in a time warp of memories, but the reality was that I had not fully grieved my mother's passing over twenty years before.

As we left Moneygall, I knew that I would never return. Suddenly out of nowhere, a Linda Hogan quotation sprang to my mind.

It gave me a sense of ease and rest, and most of all, a sense of gratitude – gratitude for my family, for those I love both here, and in the world of spirit. "Walking. I am listening to a deeper way. Suddenly, all my ancestors are behind me. Be still, they say. Watch and listen. You are the result of the love of thousands."

A Small Decent Thing

Martin Hand

Fifty-year-old married, bald, Jimmy Murphy was returning to the multi-story car park on Queen Street after his two enjoyable pints. These pints were consumed with the three surviving members of his secondary-schoolboy troop. The venue, John's Bar, was a location that thrived on neglect. It played a decent Jazzy soundtrack, for the new Dublin hipsters, in the poorest of lighting. Its dimness was only imposed to disguise the dirt of the place. Jimmy always thought that, on his visits there, he could detect the faintest stench of sewage.

In the car park, his nostrils were challenged for the second time that evening. The sharpish smell of ammonia greeted him as he passed a rough sleeper who had bedded down for the night in the stairwell.

He noticed a begging cup placed at one end of the bedding containing a few straggles of coins. Without thinking, he reached for a two-Euro coin but, in the rush to be away from the unclean spirit, he stumbled and ended up stomping on the bulk at one end of the bed.

"Ye feckin' ejit!" emerged like a banshee wail from beneath the covers.

"Sorry, Missus," was all Jimmy could muster, and he dropped the coin and scurried away.

***

In the car, Jimmy was ritually convincing himself that his driving with two pints would be unimpaired. However, the stumble of three minutes earlier laid claim to a potentially different outcome.

It was bugging him that, in trying to do a decent thing, he had come away feeling foolish. As his driving went into automatic mode, he thought about another drive maybe twenty-five or more years previously.

Carrot-headed Jimmy Murphy got the chance, one time, to do a small decent thing, and to his credit, he took it...eventually.

He was driving home from work in early April when the promise of the bright evenings to come had not yet outlived the threat of those climate-change-resilient showers – a long-winded way of saying it was cold and the ground was constantly damp.

We are talking about the early Nineties, and that's important, not only because climate change hadn't been invented then, but because sat navs hadn't either, and geography will be important in this story.

Jimmy was travelling straight down Collin's Avenue towards his right-hand turn coming into Finglas Village on Dublin's northside.

Straightforward journeys suited the twenty-something single Jimmy. He had a very un-male-like trait of being geographically challenged. This avenue was really a long residential street, and for good measure, it changed names several times along the way.

Just as Jimmy was transitioning from Glasnevin and into Finglas, a figure caught the attention of his right eye. An oldish, trenchcoat-ed man, maybe sixty yards away, was walking with short shuffling steps and clutching some sort of bulky package. He was that far away because this stretch of the road had a little ox-bow driveway in and out for residential parking.

A senior, in age, businessman Jimmy thought, carrying an awk-ward-looking briefcase. He rationalised away the peculiar unease he'd been suddenly feeling. The lights turned green, and he indicated before moving on.

***

The single dinner had been consumed but a queasiness was now immersed in his being. His mind was processing the picture. There was no distress and there was no problem, and it wasn't his anyway, and there were loads of good houses on the road, with good people in them who would surely attend to anything that wasn't quite right.

So, it took two and half hours for Jimmy to decide to make the ten-minute journey back to the scene of his own internal discomfort.

Sure enough, the senior was still there, pretty much in the same spot, shuffling along. Jimmy parked handily in the ox-bow and got himself ready to have an initial introductory chat.

The giveaway was that the bulky briefcase was in fact one of those old two-speaker radio-cassette players. Heavy buggers – the forerunner of the Ghetto Blaster.

Well, at least Jimmy was happy that returning to the scene of his crime, of omission, paid some kind of dividend.

It was eight-thirty in the evening now, the natural light was well gone. Jimmy walked un-confrontationally up to the man and asked the old boy if he needed a lift. The stranger was happy with the offer, and without any ado, they shuffled their way thirty yards back to the car, with Jimmy walking with a deliberate slowness to keep up.

They buckled up, but where to go?

'Where is it you live?' produced a stuttery story involving Churchtown. Jimmy's heart sank a bit. It was unlikely that the old man noticed his facial giveaway because he was fixed, looking straight ahead.

Jimmy was thinking, whatever about having some clue of where to go on the Northside, he had very little idea of finding locations on the Southside of Dublin. And, jeepers, how long would this trek take? He was a bit anal when it came to things like work the next day, early to bed, and all that.

Navigator Jimmy was heading due south but, in a flash of inspiration, had the sense to pull over and do a bit more investigative probing in order to avoid a complete wild goose chase.

"Would you think you'd have anything on ye that, eh...might have your address?"

Jimmy's eyes widened with a win. A buff-coloured pension book, which he instantly recognised from his own parents' possessions, so genteelly handed over. It revealed the name Richard Dowd, and an actual address in Raheny.

Now, that's better. Jimmy at least knew that the road on which he originally spotted Richard was loosely the start of the route back to that suburb. Away, the pair went again, this time in the right general direction.

Richard was trying to be a willing conversationalist but, willing or not, he revealed nothing tangible about himself. The query about how he ended up on that particular road was greeted with "the buses, the bus."

It was easy enough to discern that he was a gentle, mellow sort of a man, at least in his old age. The only tangible fact he admitted to was that he felt hungry and would eat a bit alright.

Jimmy, now more relaxed with his sense of direction, started a bit of a monologue.

"This is a bit of a quare road, Richard. Like, all the different names for the same straight street. I bet it fools all the Yanks coming from the airport in their rented cars, especially when they're reading street signs with Bóthar this and Ascaill that. You could imagine a Yank saying, "Buddie, it's a straight road, would one name not be enough? And what's wrong with English, you speak it, don't ye?" Jimmy thought all North Americans had degrees in straightforwardness.

"But, Richard, it kind of makes sense in a way, though, because this road stretches from near the seaside all the way to Corpo. Finglas. So, living close to the seaside generally means you must pay more dollars for your house. So be it. If you worked hard to get a house in a good location, then you probably played an ok and natural-enough game of distinguishing your patch from the rest. Those left behind would inherit an extra bit of swag. So, all good, Richard. What do ye think? I'll give you a gas one, Richard, though. We've passed down Glasnevin Avenue, but that used to be called Ballymun Avenue. I think a deed poll, or something, got the name changed. The thing is, Ballymun Road is far swankier but its inhabitants, it seems, never felt the need for name changes. You know, to increase the property value? Maybe they were all absentee landlords and weren't following the plot. Would you agree, Richard?"

There was no answer. Jimmy knew his limitations. At the end of the straight road, before he had to make a turn, he made a pit stop. In he went to a petrol station, to buy a street map of his own city. He knew there were twists and turns to come.

He mapped out a route from the petrol station, getting a blast of the fresh sea air through the slightly opened car window. Richard continued his silent reverie, so there would be no unwanted distractions to the mapping process.

Jimmy would only have the experience years later to realise that the poor old boy was too exhausted to talk coherently and too mannerly not to talk at all. Determined not to insult his parents' memory, perhaps.

***

Away again and it only took another fifteen minutes and two wrong turns to arrive at the terraced house door. The address was probably more impressive than the house.

Anyway, Richard waited in the car, as placid as ever, outside what seemed to be his own home. He continued to stare straight ahead, an old man in no hurry to make an escape from the sheer comfort of sitting.

No answer to the knocks on the door. What next?

Well, that's the good thing about terraced housing, you can lean across the fence to knock on the neighbour's door.

The Neighbours opened the door to a relatively late caller with a mild air of the expectation of getting news, and maybe not good news. The mam and a son, judging by appearance, were shoulder to head standing together.

"Does Richard Dowd live here?"

"Yes," the missus replied, her gaze trained diagonally past Jimmy's shoulder to see what surprise package might be in the alien white car parked outside. "Dick has been gone since yesterday morning, we think." She proceeded down her pathway, to Jimmy's relief, in a bid to interact with her neighbour.

"That's about the fourth time he's gone missing," the son explained to Jimmy. "And all the other times, the chauffeurs have been Gardaí."

He didn't bore Jimmy with the timeframe over which these expeditions into the unknown took place.

"God knows where he slept last night."

The mam had, in the meantime, managed to open the car door, undo the seatbelt, and start escorting Dick towards her own door. She reminded Jimmy of his deceased ma, and the other bingo-playing mas who were her friends on their street. Those women all shared the bond of knowing how difficult life could be and the lesson of not making it unnecessarily difficult for others.

The mam wanted to know if Jimmy wanted a call the next day.

"From the family, like?"

"No need," he said.

"What is your name, at least?"

But the small decent thing was enough.

There were a few goodbyes, and Dick seemed a bit re-energised by either the fresh air or the promise of good food. He initiated a handshake.

Deed done, and off Jimmy steered back towards the straight road, with only one wrong turn this time. Bed by eleven-thirty – not bad at all.

Jimmy never heard a word about Richard from that day. He must have driven that straight road a thousand or more times since their mini-Ulyssean odyssey together, but never heard about any new escapades Dick might have embarked upon or been rescued from.

Balding married Jimmy thought about the old man only an odd time. He had told the story once to the three buddies over the two pints. Martin was interested but Tony and Andy gave the impression of being disinterested in eccentricity.

Looking back, he was a bit surprised at how few opportunities life threw up to do small decent things.

Home now, and no checkpoints, thank God.

In Loving Memory

Emma Davis

I see you in my memories,
At the school gates with a grin.
I see you hitching in the rain,
With clothes soaked to the skin.
I see you cheer my bedside,
In a grim, hospital ward.
I see you with the family,
That you so much adored.
Could I find you now, amongst the stars,
Or upon a crescent moon,
Shining with the stolen souls,
Who were snatched away too soon?
Would I hear you whisper in the leaves,
Falling from the autumn tree?
Would you tell me in your easy voice,
That you're content and free?
Would your warm hugs wrap around me,
When the sun softens my back?
Or could you be the wildlife,
Guiding me along my track?
Don't rest in peace. Don't fade away,
Talk to me in my sleep.

Show me a sign that you are here,
So I don't have to weep.
Sit with me in your silence,
As I browse through photographs.
And reminisce on happy days,
Of your mischief, and our laughs.
I'll think of all the times we had,
Don't say this is the end.
I've so much to remember,
My affectionate, old friend.
If heaven is a state of mind,
That's where your spirit flew.
And I'll be sure to keep it safe,
It's all I have of you.
My broken heart is filled with grief,
Which nothing can appease.
But bursting through the jagged cracks,
Are loving memories.

Ghost

Leigh Kenny

She runs her fingers across the dark, burnished wood.

Not now. Not like this.

She doesn't want to see him this way. Doesn't want anyone to see her this way either, but especially not him. She lowers her gaze, long locks of golden hair falling across her face, hiding her secrets.

Hiding her pain.

She thinks of those early good times. Late nights, beer bottles, ashtrays full to overflowing with stubbed-out cigarettes. They talked for hours. Everything was so easy then.

They'd both recognised early on that they were two halves of the same creature. Maybe not the exact same, but similar enough for them to feel that cosmic pull, that invisible thread that seemed to bind them, pull them into each other's orbit.

She remembers the first time – that first forbidden foray into physical touch. Giving in to that lust after so long was like nothing she had ever felt before. In her young life, she'd heard people speak of the 'earth moving' in movies and books so many times, but that night it really had. She still remembers that gentle shift, like the stars themselves were realigning to ensure they both knew that the universe itself wanted this.

Needed this.

Needed them.

Heat creeps into her cheeks, flushing her face as she reminisces.

The pain that came next. The fights and the silences. The mourning.

How hard it had been then to mourn a person who wasn't dead.

He was to be a ghost to her, although she was the real ghost – a phantom draped in darkness and tumult, haunting her own dreams and rattling the chains of what was, what could have been.

So many years of darkness until, finally, the universe favoured them again, and her world became a rainbow of colour and texture once more. Laughter, shared jokes, knowing looks between two people who felt as though nothing existed in the cosmos around them. Days in the long grass, shoulder to shoulder, counting stars they could not see but knew existed. For how could those pinpricks of dancing light not exist in a world so beautiful and full of magic?

Nights by the water, beneath the shadow of the old lighthouse, the light dancing on the crests of waves while his fingers danced across her skin. The wind blew cold for that time of year, but the fire within her – within them both – ignited in a blaze of need and passion.

Until the universe decided it wanted something different of her.

She did its bidding and followed the path laid out.

Became a ghost again.

This time, she was not as haunted, for she had the memories to wrap herself in, like a protective shroud to remind her that their time would come again.

Until it couldn't.

Time had run out.

And here she now sat before him, pulled again by that invisible thread woven by forces bigger than either of them – its only goal to bring them together once more. One final time to say goodbye.

She swallows hard – tears stinging her eyes and blurring her vision – and sways as she finds her feet. She reaches into the coffin and brushes his cheek with her fingertips. The parlour lights dance across his waxen face, his eyes never to look upon her again. She turns from the wooden box that contains only skin and bone, sinew and satin. That body doesn't house the real him any more than the coffin does. He only lives in memories now – in the past and in the what ifs. In the foaming waves of a moonlit sea and the scattered dust among stars the eye could not behold.

He will always be almost hers.

She leaves, invisible to all, wrapped in a new shroud of grief and regret.

A ghost for the rest of her days.

She is her own haunting.

The Loop

D.C. Spuera

Blood dripped from Ciaran's nose and mouth, leaving a trail as he crawled across the wooden floor, his once-clean and crisp white shirt stained red.

"Thank you, Master, that was brilliant! Brilliant! Did you see their faces? That bitch Christina, how I hate her. And Scott, oh my 'best friend forever'. That backstabber. Oh, they looked so happy, thinking they were so rich now. Poor little Ciaran, they thought, rich but stupid."

"Master, I have given you two dark souls, as promised. That was a good trade. Those two weeks with my husband were the best, living life to the fullest and closing my life story in style and grace.

"I can never thank you enough. This is the best day of my life." Ciaran laughed as blood spewed again from his mouth.

"Actually, it is the best day of my death."

***

Scott arrived first at the big house; the door was open. "Hello. Hello. Is anyone home? Ciaran, are you home?"

"Just getting changed, Scott," Ciaran called from upstairs. "Down in a minute. Help yourself to the whiskey – ice is in the bucket."

"Thanks." He helped himself to a crystal glass of whiskey and ice. Ciaran's house was something else: opulent and gaudy. Little prick!

The front doorbell sounded.

"Can you get that for me, Scott? It will be Christina."

Scott made his way to the door and opened it. It had been fifteen years since he'd seen Christina, and she looked as beautiful as ever.

They exchanged 'air kisses' before he took her fake fur coat in a gentlemanly way. "Want a whiskey and ice? It looks expensive."

"Sure, why not."

He remembered how stunning she was at school – she still was – and tried to hide his lustful glances at the cleavage on display. Christina grabbed him close, her mouth to his ear.

"What in the name of Jesus are we doing here, Scott? I haven't seen or heard from this little shit in fifteen years. Then, out of the blue, this invitation and a cheque for ten thousand euros to 'cover expenses'. What is going on? Do you know?"

Scott shrugged, then turned around as Ciaran walked down the stairs, buttoning his tailor-made white shirt.

"Christina. Scott. So good to see you again. Thank you for coming. Please, sit down – we have so much to catch up on. Scott, give Christina a shot of the whiskey, and I will have one too. It is Midleton. Very Rare – twenty-ten. It cost me over two thousand in auction, but it is worth every euro."

All three sat at the table.

"This may seem odd," Ciaran said, opening the conversation, "but I wanted to talk to you about something important. You probably don't know this, but you were the most influential people in my life as a young man. If it had not been for you, Scott, I wouldn't have learned never to trust anyone, especially in business. As for you, Christina, I would still be hiding my sexuality and would never have met and married Mark."

Scott tried to hide his surprise. He thought he would be the last person Ciaran would thank.

"Just in case you are wondering," Ciaran continued, "Mark has returned to his home in Washington, and I gave the house staff the day off. I wanted to share some news with you, confidentially. I am dying."

All three took an embarrassed sip of whiskey to let that sink in. Scott mumbled something about being sorry before he hid behind his crystal glass again.

"Cancer. Doctors give me between three weeks and three months. I am not sad. I have lived a good life, I have loved, and I have seen the world. And now, dear friends, I want to thank you both. You helped me become who I am today. I will be eternally grateful."

Scott and Christina exchanged glances, and Scott assumed they were both thinking the same thing: Let's get out of here, far away from this freak.

Ciaran seemed not to notice. "But I want to repay you with more than just a glass of expensive whiskey and a simple thank you. So I took the liberty of drawing up some documentation – an addendum to my Last Will and Testament, so to speak."

He handed them a single sheet of paper each and sat back as they read it. At first, nothing was said. Then Scott mumbled "Holy shit" before continuing. As both finished reading, they looked up.

Ciaran gave them a warm smile. "Yes, it reads correctly. Scott, when I die, I am handing you ownership of my companies to continue or sell as you see fit. And, Christina, you get this house and the apartment in Washington to sell or do whatever you like with. The companies are valued at three-point-two million combined, and the properties are close to three million. When I die, you will both be millionaires."

Scott poured all three another Midleton. It was unbelievable. Please, God, let it be three weeks and not three months they both thought.

Ciaran smiled. "All you need to do is sign the papers. I will countersign and take a picture using my phone, and my solicitor will log it as an attachment to my will immediately. Signed and sealed."

Scott read over the paper again, just in case there was something sneaky in there that he'd missed. One thing stood out.

"Ciaran, it says here that in the event of my death, the companies, or any proceeds from the sale of the companies that are left, will be passed on to my two boys. Why did you do that?"

Ciaran smiled again, then took a sip before placing his glass on the table. "Finding you two guys took me a while. For you, Scott, it was easy enough. You have always been money-driven and own many investment companies, although they seem to come and go very quickly. I also see that you and Mary-Anne are divorced now, and she has sole custody of the two boys. I always had a soft spot for Mary-Anne. You left her for your secretary. What was her name?"

"Trisha."

"Ah yes, Trisha, she was very pretty. Quite young too."

Scott smirked. When Trisha turned twenty-one, he'd kicked her out. He preferred younger girls now. Much, much younger.

He took up the paper again, signed his name, and handed it back to Ciaran. Ciaran countersigned it. He lifted his iPhone, took a picture, typed some words, and showed it to Scott.

"Done. When I die, you will inherit both companies straight away. Can I suggest you take a picture and send it to your solicitor, if you have one, so there can be no mistake?"

Scott complied right away, unable to hold in a smile that felt like it reached from ear to ear. Money left from the sale of the two companies to go to his boys and that bitch Mary-Anne? Ha, no way – he would spend it like it was tap water.

Ciaran's face brightened with what could only be described as a disarming smile. "It was a bit harder to find you, Christina, but once I established that you were in the adult movie business, finding you did not take long. I love that name, Angel Delight. Reminds me of Sunday afternoon lunch desert."

Hate burned in Christina's eyes but vanished in a microsecond. A girl does what she is good at, and if she can make a living from it, so be it. She was a movie star, maybe not mainstream, but the money was good, and she enjoyed the sex. Now, she was having much more fun working with the Eastern European gangs, breaking in the new girls they smuggled into the country. The look on their faces when she took them to their first 'cleaning' job! She snatched up the pen and signed her name. Ciaran countersigned, took a picture with a few words added, and sent it.

"Good – that is done. In case you missed it, Christina, in the event of your death, the house and apartments, or anything left from their sale, will go to your sister, Deidre. She was a good friend to me through the tough times at school."

Christina didn't care. She would make sure that the milksop of a sister of hers got nothing.

"I hope you don't mind, but I put a bottle of two thousand and eight Dom Pérignon champagne on ice for the occasion. Scott, would you be so kind as to open it and pour us three glasses? I am exhausted. Doctor says I should not drink, but what's the worst it can do, kill me?"

Everyone laughed, especially Ciaran.

Three crystal champagne glasses clinked together and were drained simultaneously.

"Another."

"Why did you do this?" Scott asked, the whiskey and champagne releasing his guarded tongue. "I thought you hated us both? Why give us all that money?"

Ciaran sat back in his chair, a contented look on his face.

"Oh, but I did. No, correction: I *do* hate you both. You destroyed my life. You, Scott, I thought we were best friends for life. But when we got older, you started to run with the Malloys. They bullied and beat me at every opportunity, stealing my dinner money every day. You just laughed. You were my friend – I trusted you. It nearly broke me.

"And you, Christina, remember the day you took me to the tool-shed at the back of Malloy's farm? You told me you were going to make a man out of me. I was only fifteen. You stripped me naked and demanded sex. Then, when I couldn't get aroused, you laughed at me and said I was pathetic. You told the whole school about it. You and your friends graffitied it everywhere. Ciaran is gay, Ciaran likes boys, Ciaran sucks... You remember? Everyone laughed at me, beat me even more, and made my life a misery. But the worst was when my da found out from his mates in the pub. They all laughed at him. He came home drunk and took his belt to me and ma that night."

Scott and Christina sat back. "So why did you give us all this money?" Scott asked.

Ciaran smiled. "Because I did not want to take all this cold hate to the grave with me. What is the point of that? I forgive you both."

Scott jumped up. "You forgive us? That is so big of you! You in your fancy house, looking down on us, with your gay American friends, thinking you are so high and mighty. You forgive us...? We don't forgive you! You disgust us, both of us. And I tell you now, every cent you leave us will be spent having the time of our lives, squandering it without a care in the world."

Ciaran put on a sad facial expression. "Is that how you feel as well, Christina?"

"I remember that time in the shed, Ciaran. I offered you the full extent of my womanhood, and you couldn't even be bothered to rise to the occasion. You are truly pathetic. Yes, I wrote those things, for I didn't want anyone to think it was my fault."

Ciaran took another drink of his champagne and sighed. "I am sorry you feel that way, but I suppose it was inevitable. Nevertheless, I picked myself up, Scott, and opened my first software company, then several more. I made millions. Christina, it may not have been the way I wanted to come out to my parents about being gay, but to be honest, I might not have had the courage to do so. But it became easier for me once I recognized who I was. I met and married Mark, and we had a good life together. So, no matter what you think, you both shaped my life for the better, to where it is today. So, thank you."

All three sat back, for the whole thing was exhausting. Ciaran took a moment, sat forward, and looked at them both.

"Oh, I have good news and bad news. First, the good news. You will not have to wait three months, or even three weeks, to inherit after my death. I am dying this very night. In a short while, it will be all yours. You always said you wanted to be a millionaire, Scott, so after tonight, you will be. And, Christina, you will be famous for being the wealthiest adult film star in all of Ireland.

Christina and Scott were shocked, but that soon turned to excitement at getting their hands on Ciaran's wealth – maybe even tomorrow. They hugged each other in happiness. Then Scott realised what Ciaran had said. "I am sorry you are dying so soon. At least you get to spend your last evening with us."

Ciaran looked tired, and he took a long drink of his champagne.

"Yes, I am glad we could be together tonight. Dying alone is so heartbreaking. It's good to be surrounded by friends."

Scott took his hand, and Christina pulled Ciaran into her warm, ample bosom.

"We are here for you, Ciaran," she said. "So how will you end it tonight – stop all the pain and suffering?"

"I am glad you asked that. I thought about hanging myself, but that is such an ugly way to die. Then I thought about a shotgun to the head, but we just got the new sofa last week, and the stains would never come out. So, I decided to end it with dignity and a touch of class. I poisoned the Dom Pérignon champagne."

Silence hung over the room. Scott looked at the empty bottle of champagne, his gaze then drawn to the empty glass – all three empty glasses.

A drop of blood left his nose, causing a pretty red blob to appear on the wooden floor.

Christina screamed and grabbed Ciaran by the shirt, then doubled over and rolled gracefully to the floor. Scott crumpled on top of her.

Ciaran fell to the floor, dripping blood, crawling away from them both.

***

"Master, I beg you, can we replay it all again? Just once more. This will be the last time, I promise."

A dark, menacing voice clawed its way out of the darkness.

"You got your extra two weeks, and you want it all again? You really are greedy, aren't you? Did you know this will be the six hundred and sixty-sixth time we have repeated this? Okay then, just once more."

Ciaran raised his hands in the air, about to say, "Thank you", but the words were never released – his last breath taken over by his death rattle.

Evil laughter bounced from floor to ceiling in the dark, empty house.

***

Scott arrived first at the big house; the door was open. "Hello. Hello. Is anyone home? Ciaran, are you home...?"

My First Car

Betty O'Mahony

When I was nineteen years old, I bought my first car. A second-hand blue Fiat 500 with a sunroof. I loved that car. It was temperamental and spent a lot of time at the garage for essential repairs, but it was perfect in my eyes, and I told myself it was just teething trouble.

My husband used to play guitar, banjo, and mandolin so we would go to a lot of music sessions all over Cork City and County. One of the favourite destinations was Crookhaven in West Cork – Billy O'Sullivan's pub if you are familiar with the area. A beautiful coastline welcomed you the entire way to Crookhaven from Goleen and the sun always shone. The area is so beautiful that everything and everyone shines in the warmth of the welcome that lies waiting for you there.

One time, on the way into Crookhaven, all the cars were stopped by the local sergeant doing a check for tax and insurance. He was taken with my little car and had a good look at the tyres, wing-mirrors and so on, then waved us on with a pleasant smile.

That evening my husband was playing in the pub with other musicians and a great singsong was in full throttle. The entire pub joined in the singing, and it nearly lifted the roof with the power of the songs! There was a huge crowd there and many other musicians and singers as well, so we all had a wonderful time. The tourists were charmed with it all. At closing time Billy, the owner of the pub, was trying to clear the place to no avail, and after a while the sergeant appeared in the doorway. He stood therefor a few seconds searching the room and everyone stopped singing and waited to see what he was going to do. Then he spotted me and walked straight over.

"Your car is gone," he whispered into my ear.

That galvanised me into action and I shot out the door at a run, with my husband holding the musical instruments, at full speed behind me. I always had to park the car on a hill to get it started – it was one of its little peccadillos, so I ran up the hill at a sprint. Of course, the session was over now, and Billy and the sergeant were delighted. My car was parked in the usual spot, to my relief, and I ran back downhill and over to the sergeant to tell him.

He burst out laughing saying it was the only way he had to stop the music. "I had to clear the pub," he said.

We all joined in with the laughter. I had to admire him for thinking outside the box! West Cork had its own rules in those days and life ticked on at a slower pace.

My lovely first car broke down a lot and as a result I got to know the wonderful people of West Cork extremely well. They never let us down. You would always be taken care of, and always got lots of advice, of course. It was a surprise to learn that everyone took a half day in Bantry on a Wednesday. I discovered that while searching for a mechanic after the car broke down yet again. The clutch cable had broken.

"No problem," said one of the citizens of Bantry and they found someone to replace the clutch cable with the usual generosity of spirit of the West Cork inhabitants. "Sure, it's no trouble at all," was the usual mantra. How could you fail to fall in love with these people? You could almost taste the benevolence in the atmosphere.

My most memorable escapade was when I believed the little car could take on anything. I was driving out of Bantry onetime and got stuck behind an articulated truck. He was driving neither fast nor slowly, and I thought I'll pass him out on the straight bit just outside Bantry. There was nothing coming towards me, so I set off. I got halfway down the truck when I realised I could get no farther – there just wasn't enough power in the engine – so I had to slide back behind the truck again.

I tried a second time at the next straight stretch, but the same thing happened, and again I had to pullback. I had a big red face by now and the driver of the artic kept waving at me as I disappeared behind him. At the next straight stretch of road, the artic driver pulled over to the hard shoulder and slowed enough to let me pass, which I eventually managed to do, and then he came back on the road behind me and serenaded me with his powerful sound system, waving and giving me the thumbs-up sign. That experience made me realise the limits of my little car.

Limits or not it was a lovely car, and they were wonderful times. Hap-hap-hap-hap-happy days.

My Grandfather

John Joe McGinley

We walked that path, my hand in yours,
Beside the sea and rocky shores,
The air was sweet with salt and pine,
Your voice a steady, gentle line.
The world was wide, but you were near,
A shield against my smallest fear,
As waves crashed far and gulls flew high,
You taught me how to watch the sky.
The rocks beneath, worn and grey,
Yet in your stories, they would play,
Tales of ships and sailors bold,
Of things the ocean never told.
Your laughter mingled with the breeze,
And I, so small, could walk with ease,
For every step with you was light,
The world felt soft, and time was bright.
Now years have passed, and tides have turned,
The path grown faint, the grasses burned,
Yet in my mind, you're walking still,
Along that path, beyond the hill.
The sea may change, the winds may die,
But in my heart, you never say goodbye.

Lucky Lucas

David Bowmore

Lucas landed on the wooden boards, accompanied by shattering glass, a high-pitched scream, and a bullet destined for woodwork on the other side of Main Street. He buckled his gun belt in place as he scooted along the narrow first-floor veranda which ran round the edge of the saloon. No point in shooting back. Seth, the big lumbering oaf, would never get through the window in time. Once around the corner, he vaulted over the railings, landing lightly in the sand, barely out of breath. With Seth's curses ringing in his ears, he made his way along the backs of buildings until he reached the stables on the edge of town. By morning, he would be far away, buying a seat in another poker game.

Lucas had always been lucky.

***

Lucas rode back into town between two tall posts that had once supported the 'Welcome to Tumbleweed' signboard. As he made his way along Main Street, he peered through the walls of the wooden buildings where the planks had given way, looking for signs of life. Sunlight glinted off broken glass in many of the windows, and grass struggled to grow on sand that had gathered in high drifts, obliterating boardwalks. The only living creature he saw was a single lizard basking in the midday sun on the jailhouse door.

Outside the saloon, he looped the horse's reins over the hitching rail; the trough underneath empty and dry, save for dust and dead flies. The horse looked at him with one large, sad eye, whinnying when he rubbed her nose.

He pushed on the saloon doors and stepped inside, removed his old, battered hat and proceeded to brush away dirt and sand. A couple of tables lay on their sides, and an upright piano stood in the corner. He wandered over to it, boots thumping on the boards. After raising the key lid, he played a quick tune to get the attention of anyone who might be crazy enough to still live in the town.

As suspected, no one answered the off-key call.

Lucas ran a finger along the dusty layer on the bar top. At least the mirror behind was in one piece, albeit badly mottled. He spun, left hand dropping to his holster, at the sound of the key lid dropping into place over the ivory.

No one there, except those his memory conjured up. Accompanied by an old soak at the piano who played for beer, delicious Mary wore a charming Parisian dress – all feathers, bustle, and cleavage – and sang a song about Dublin town. Many wanton eyes watched her hit the high-note finale as she clasped her hands beneath her bosom. Lucas turned his attention to the game, to his hand, but knowing what was on the cards later forced an unwise call. With the hand lost, he threw in the cards and went to lean at the bar. Ordering whiskey from the aproned bartender, he slid two bits across the shining surface, and watched Mary's reflection glide around the room to the stairs that led up to the bedrooms. Pausing for an extra second, her gaze met his in the mirror.

Glass crunched underfoot as he searched behind the bar, looking for anything to ease his thirst, to no avail. The vision at the end of the counter shimmered, revealing itself to be Seth, innkeeper of one of the best bars this side of the Red River. For a wife, he had one of the fairest ladies a chancer was ever likely to see up close, let alone be lucky enough to take a tumble with. Lucas would have bet over the odds that Seth would never have found a woman like Mary in ten lifetimes. But she had pitched up, looking for a fresh start away from the hookshops of San Francisco. And back then, Seth had money. Lots of money.

A check of the rooms upstairs found them to be deserted, with the exception of a few mouldering clothes in wardrobes and tattered curtains that blew in the glassless windows. A waistcoat hung over one of the brass bed knobs. He slipped once-nimble fingers into a pocket, and pulled out a beautifully engraved silver pocket watch. After looking it over, he set the time and wound the mechanism. It ticked. He smiled, placing it back in the pocket.

He saw her on the bed, skirts pulled up to reveal long, luscious legs and a welcoming shadow. Half an hour with Mary was worth the wrath of her husband's well-known fiery temper.

But her eyes. Lucas, do not forget her eyes. How could he ever forget those glittering pools?

He should never have gone back for her the day after his lucky escape. But the thought of Seth's big brutish hands punishing her – cracking ribs, bruising flesh, and bringing tears to those lovely eyes – brought out his gallant side. He told himself the hand had already been dealt, there was nothing else to play for. But foolishly, believing he could save Mary, perhaps even give her a better life, he made his call.

As he stood in the bathhouse across Main Street, he observed a long-dead rat in one of the tin baths. Knowing it wouldn't work, but hoping for a lucky break, he pulled on the iron pump's ornate handle. Nothing came out except stale air. He tried again and brought forth a trickle of brown liquid. With hope in the air, he kept pumping until the water ran clear. He and his horse would not die of thirst. Not today.

Since they were children, he had always pushed his luck, and Seth always struck first.

After the ruckus, Lucas woke many miles from Tumbleweed, shaded from the blistering sun by the long branches of a lone mesquite tree, a bloody hole in his shoulder. And, somehow, he had survived.

He picked up the reins, put a foot in the stirrup, heaved himself into the saddle with an aged groan – the old bullet wound still throbbed when rain was in the air – and headed out of town.

A mile south lay the graveyard. Mary's wooden cross had fallen forward in the dry soil. He straightened it before doing the same for Seth's marker.

If he could play the hand again, he'd fold rather than call.

Lucas had always been lucky.

The Importance Of The Consistent

Fiona Gill

You're the reliable,
The one with an open door policy,
The one that's always happy to see me.
You take out the cups, and the place mats,

You sit me on his chair and tell me it's fine.
You unplug the radio, so the chatter quietens,
You fill the kettle with fresh water
And click, as it steams and bubbles.
You busy yourself by the biscuit tin,
All the while asking ...
What has brought me in?
You sit, opposite, eyes fixed, ears ready and ... exhale,
You enquire, but give time.

You pour the tea into the perfect mug,
You pour the milk from the tiny jug,
You push across the silver, sugar bowl
And place the tiny spoon down beside it.
You let me think, and speak, and find a rhythm,
Willing to laugh at any vain attempt at a joke,
You surprise yourself with a giggle

when I actually say a good quip,

You give time
Like you've no one else to tend to.
You have an open heart
And a joy in the art of conversation,
You always remembered,
Made it your mission
To make every significant date unmissable.
You were instrumental in the human I have become,
You made me feel that I always belonged.

A shield, a shelter, a space, always so full of care.
You gave me so much,
It's hard to match words to,
But I am the luckiest human
To have known you.

Written in loving memory of
My Gran, Pauline Gill.

Chestnut Heaven

Eoin Brady

Dawn quenched the limpet moon. A turning tide of mist flowed from the valley in rivulets that eddied to the course and currents of forgotten rivers, carrying away flotsam of dreams, the lost stanzas in night's unpublished poems. A sunken cloud hid the dew-drop jewels of morning from the warming cotton tinder sky.

It was into this, Dad woke me with a whispered "The chestnuts have fallen." Spoken as if they'd hear him and startle.

I jumped from bed already dressed and snuck the currant buns outside to place by the shed, making noise enough to let the world know I was there. Then I hid in the long grass, scattering mist like sleepy sheep. Lacing green strands between my fingers, I wove myself to the earth so as not to slip into the oceans of fading stars above. Then I waited.

Hearing the shed door open, I felt the kind of contentment reserved for children. When it closed, I was up running, and barrelled into the door, then stretched to reach the rusted bolt before worrying it shut. Silence made me doubt, but the sharp chime of Mam's bike bell called me to breakfast.

"What divilment has you grinning?"

I could not stop laughing, so I filled my gob with porridge and buried my secret beneath a clump of strawberry jam. Dad conducted the morning rituals with the habitual 'ting-ting' of his razor against the sink's edge.

Roosts emptied as crows raced Mam to town. Dad left a wake of straw behind his tractor to follow – if need be. Later, I had my lunch, gathered empty bags, and the promise they would be full by teatime.

The shed bolt shrieked when I opened it. Inside, a stack of summering logs was now a loom of cobwebs. Atop a store of coal was a nest of scratchy bags and painting rags, which were of better quality than those worn by the little girl inside it. Fat tears cleared pink streaks down her gaunt, filthy cheeks.

"How come you're living in the shed? There's spiders in here." I stepped closer, but not in. That's how the spiders got you.

"I'm sorry."

"Oh, I didn't mean to scare you. Will you still grant my wish? I caught you fairly."

She pressed up against the back wall, cradling a chubby finger in her fist.

"Don't need to be afraid. You're a Chancesmith, aren't you? Here, look, I didn't eat all the sweets, in case you wanted some.' I offered her my lunchbox. 'Gave you the buns, too." I left out that it was because I hated currants.

"What's a Chancesmith?"

"Granda used to say if you catch one, they give you a wish. They don't do chores or have bedtimes. No parents to listen to."

She perked up at that. "I want to be a Chancesmith."

We devoured the sweets first. She smelled of outside, and her skeleton arms reminded me of dark stories; fury in the deep cairns crushed by year-long winters. But her feet kicked when the sticky flesh of the jellies melted into sugar and happiness, setting me at ease.

"I have to find Chestnut Heaven. Do you want to help?"

She nodded.

"Cool. Let's go conker hunting!"

I gave her one of Granda's jackets. It hung below her brittle knees, but stopped her shivering. Afraid I'd lose her, I held her hand through fields and over the warbling walls by the ringfort that was still lit by the cold light of golden lichen. Old forgetful moss along the river never held prints for long, but she could. There was one direction she refused to go.

In a hidden copse, we searched beneath gnarled leaves from last season. They were the colour of aged autumn and crinkled underfoot, delicate as dandelions.

"I found one!' Her body shook with pride.

"Wow! That's deadly! Put it in your bag."

"You have it."

"No. Finders keepers."

"Is this Chestnut Heaven?"

"I don't remember. Granda never told me where it was, and he died, so I haven't seen him in a while."

Our pockets full of rich mahogany – the currency of youth – I forgot the wish until she asked if she had one too.

"Yeah! Well. Don't you?"

Her face fell, as if she already knew the answer.

"What do you want?"

"Can we pick more chestnuts?"

"Yeah! Why do you always say sorry all the time?"

"I don't know."

"That's silly. If you say sorry, the adults will know you did it. "Sorry is a last resort," Granda used to say, but Mam made him say sorry for telling me that."

We followed hunger home and squirrelled our treasure at the back door. Mam brought the birds to chatter.

"Well, yous were easy to find. Just listen for all the laughing."

My friend grew quiet. Every word a prize hard-won. Mam could only make out her name was Nora, and she was a Chancesmith.

Mam made dinner, with all the nice things you only saw on one plate at Christmas. We ate by the garden stream and watched the last showing of pond skaters dance across sunset.

Even though I was on my best behaviour, Mam was annoyed. She ran a bath in silence. I took the side with the cold taps and hoarded bubbles like precious pearls.

Nora would not take the jacket off and refused to let go of her chestnut, so Mam cleaned her with a warm cloth. Every gentle touch made her flinch and whimper. Mam dabbed delicately, soaking uptears while removing Nora's mask with cooing, soothing susurrations. I couldn't understand why Mam cried too. Some of the coal dust did not wash away. It stained deep into Nora's skin. Yellow as harsh smoke in places.

Nora held Mam's arm, begging her not to take away the day. "Please! I want to be a Chancesmith."

Dad's humming warmed the house.

"Dáithí! Come here to me!"

Dad took the stairs two at a time. He beamed at Nora, but then something strange happened. I'd never seen a smile wilt before. "Hello."

"I'm sorry," Nora said.

Mam's teeth chattered so much, I wondered if they'd shatter. "Where are you going?"

"I know of her father." Dad's walk backdown was pensive and reminded me of lazy church incense ghosts and how delicately he stepped when he shouldered his father beneath a cairn of wood, brass, and memories.

"Don't ever call him that in my house," Mam said.

I didn't understand, but I knew then that I would never see my grandad again.

Over the years, wind, rain, and winters wore away at the coal shed. I remember the best of that time vaguely. Each morning, I try recapture the taste of my childhood, but the memory of my mother's porridge lingers just beyond reach. The gentle bell of my father's shaving went quiet for me long before I took up the tune. What magic the chestnuts held faded along with Nora's glamour of coal dust. Forgotten, the seeds took root and now the garden is shaded by a copse of tall chestnut trees.

When I walk beneath their boughs, the crows pay no mind to my pocket-filling. I feel like a man that left home never to return and planted these seeds in a new country as an alter to the old. Invasive nostalgia, connecting me to a place, time, and people I will never see again.

A Summer Fair

Catherine Kullmann

"I met him once, you know."

Anna paused the film and turned to stare at her grandmother. "You did what, *Oma*?"

Her grandmother smiled, "It's true. In nineteen fifty-nine, at the *Johanneskirmes*, one of the biggest summer fairs in Hesse. People came from miles around, including lots of G.I.s from the American barracks, all eager to talk to the *Fräuleins*.

"My friend Christa and I were both seventeen and had just finished our first year at Commercial College. The next year, we would qualify as secretaries. We both had new dresses – hers was pink and mine blue – with white polka dots, and white belts, collars, and cuffs. We had stiffened our slips with sugar water to support the full skirts – oh, we thought we were the bee's knees!

"The *Amis* were very different to the German boys we knew from school and dancing class. They were older, very smart in their dress uniforms, and smelled of American cigarettes, spearmint chewing gum, and the colognes and pomades they used on their close-shaven cheeks and short hair. They didn't ask if they might accompany us, but walked beside us, with smiles and '*Hi, Fräuleins*', and sort of drifted in among us girls so that, before we knew it, we had split up into couples. By the time we reached the fairground, we were a group of twelve – six German girls and six *Amis*.

"My G.I. was called Hank. He was blond with broad shoulders, blue eyes, and a crooked smile, and he spoke with a sexy drawl. You could imagine him as a cowboy in a movie. He knew some German – his grandparents were from Germany – and I had worked hard at my English, so we could talk together better than most of the other couples.

"As we neared the fairgrounds, we could hear the oompah-pah-pah of the brass band and girls shrieking as their boys tugged hard on the ropes so the swing-boats went right up to the bar. And then there was that fairground smell: *Bratwurst*, candyfloss, sizzling potato cakes, burnt almonds, and sweet fried dough, all mixed with the oily smell of hot engines and the heavy scent of the linden trees that shaded one end of the grounds." She laughed. "Even today, when I smell it, I am seventeen again.

"We strolled through the lanes between the booths, talking and laughing, and we stopped to watch a puppet show – the *Amis* laughed as much as the children at the antics of *Kasperle* and his crew. Of course, they had to have a go at the shooting-stand. They didn't do too badly, but then Ilse came up and beat them all. They couldn't believe it. She won a teddy-bear, which she insisted on presenting to her G.I., just the way a boy would give his prize to a girl. So he had to carry it the whole time.

"We tried the chair-o-planes and the swing-boats, and then we all got into the bumper cars and whizzed around the floor, crashing into each other until we were dizzy, our throats dry from screaming. As soon as we stopped, we headed to the tables and benches near the bandstand for an apple spritzer or a beer. I felt so grown-up. It was the first time I had been allowed stay so late. In previous years, I had to go home once the afternoon band stopped playing.

"I was mortified when Willi got up on the stage. He wasn't a bad singer, but so old-fashioned. The *Amis* seemed to like our folk songs, though, and clapped and hummed along with everyone else. Willi's last song was '*Muss i denn, muss i denn zum Städele hinaus?*'

"'What language was that?' Hank asked afterwards. 'I couldn't understand a word.'

"'It's Swabian dialect', I told him. 'An apprentice has passed his journeyman exams and now must leave town to work elsewhere for a year. He is saying goodbye to his sweetheart, promising to remain true to her. They'll marry if she still loves him when he returns.'

"'Like us,' one of the G.I.s said. 'Do you know it? Sing it again.'

"So we girls sang and they hummed along. The second time, they made a stab at the chorus. It was a real tongue twister for them, and the people around us laughed, but not unkindly.

"'Let's try that caterpillar ride,' one of the boys said. So off we went. I was a little nervous because, well, when the hood closed over the little carriages—"

"Hank might kiss you," her granddaughter offered. "Was it your first kiss, *Oma*?"

"*Ja*. He was nice – didn't try to maul me or anything like that. Afterwards, he bought me a gingerbread heart on a ribbon to hang around my neck. Then the dance music started. They weren't all used to our sort of dancing – there was no swing or rock and roll – but they soon got the hang of it. Hank was a good dancer. He held you properly – not too tight but firm enough that it was easy to follow him. It grew dark, and strings of lanterns were lit. I didn't want the evening to end, but I had to be home by midnight and the boys had to be back at the base by then too. So, about a quarter-past-eleven, Christa and her G.I., and Hank and I took a cab to our home – it wasn't very far but too far for them to walk us home before heading for the base. Christa's boy started to hum '*Muss i denn*', and we all joined in.

"They saw us to the door. There was just time for another quick kiss before my father opened it. They said '*auf Wiedersehen*' and the night was over.

"And that," she said as she picked up the remote, "is how Christa Hartmann and I taught your grandfather and Elvis Presley the melody and chorus of *Wooden Heart*."

This story is completely fictional, as are the characters, except for Elvis himself. He was stationed in Germany between October 1958 and March 1960 during his military service. The melody and original German chorus of Muss i denn, muss i denn zum Städele hinaus? were used for the song Wooden Heart in the 1960 film G. I. Blues. My story was written in response to a prompt for a story inspired by a song.

Spare Parts

Anne McDonald

I keep my mother's handwriting near me as I write.
Sealed tight in a plastic pocket, now slightly faded,
containing a neat, precise request.
"Please forward Whirlpool spare part, Model 882,
One Grey, Rubber, New.
Thanking You,
Peggy Faulkner."
Handwriting for the return address is elegant, cursive, blue ink.
She didn't think as she wrote her note,
that she was out of time for spare parts,
or inscribing Holy Communion books or birthday cards,
or writing letters to her cousin in the States.
By the time the doctors got to her, it was too late.

A stroke, or stroke of luck (bad),
ripped away the confident hand, left one that trembled,
replaced her speech with mumbles,
brain damage, permanent, severe, no possible repair.
No spare parts department for us to contact.

It was never meant to happen to her.
No model number for parts required,

no customer service for a brain rewired all wrong.
Life changed forever overnight. The mam we knew was long gone.
"*Get Well*" cards were tired and trite.

No "please forward" no, "thanking you" as we trawled through things
to reconnect her with us, and us with her.
No calls by phone, no going home, ever.

I keep my mother's handwriting beside me as I write,
so I remember who she was before it all got broken.

An Open Wound

Eamon O'Cleirigh

The driving rain flowed in rivulets from Barry's golf umbrella. His leather shoes were mucked up and soaked, as were his trousers below the knees but he didn't care. What bothered him was much deeper than the rain-soaked graveyard verge he stood on. Ten metres away, a plywood board topped the entrance to his mother's grave, the mound of freshly dug earth to the side covered by a well-used green cloth that had seen better days.

Four workmen were now at the far side of the graveyard, their pace gathering as they approached their cinder-block office, no doubt eager to get out of the downpour and their wets, a hot cuppa a just reward for a duty met in harsh conditions.

Barry's back teeth ground almost to breaking point at the thought of what was going to happen, and at the absolute injustice that faced him. He took a deep, slow breath to steady himself. It was still early – nine-forty. The Mass took place at ten-thirty, so they wouldn't arrive at the graveyard before twelve. Not even two and a half hours before his mother's resting place, her memory – her remains – would be defiled forever.

He stood now beside the plot and recalled how, fifteen years before, her coffin had been lowered into the grave with her feet where the headstone would be. It had seemed so odd then how he was the only one who noticed, and that nobody was bothered when he voiced it later in the pub. Wasn't it a given that a person should be buried with their head where the gravestone would be? What's the point in talking to a person's feet while visiting their grave? And why the hell didn't it bother anyone else in the family?

And why was their bastard of a father due to be lowered into their mother's grave in a couple of hours' time? And why was he the only one to object? Hadn't they known the same man? Experienced the same life? Witnessed the abuse he'd doled out to his long-suffering wife?

Maybe it was down to him being a man among women – the only boy in the family – the youngest, and closest to their mother. While the girls had to know what was going on, that man was still 'their Daddy', the one who'd sent them to the best schools, bought them the best clothes, and ensured they were active in the best sports and youth groups.

It had been the same with him – he'd seen it all, but obviously more than them. He'd stopped talking to his father in his thirteenth year. On arriving home from kickboxing, a twice-weekly afterschool activity, he'd found his mother in the kitchen crying into a teacloth. He'd been looking forward to a 'free house' for the few days ahead – they all were – with his parents' plan to attend a wedding in Portugal.

With his mother almost hysterical, it took ages to coax the cause out of her, the woman's heartbroken sobs pulling his own tears from a vault he'd thought tightly locked. When she calmed enough to reveal the truth, he sat back and just nodded, unsurprised by the actions of a man he'd observed sneaking women into the house while his mother was out working.

This time, his father had returned home, an hour before they were due to depart, with the news that work had come up which he couldn't ignore, and he wouldn't be back for a week or so. Barry was pretty confident he'd find the man in Portugal if he were to make the trip, and that he'd have one of his floozies on his arm.

He'd simply not spoken to the man after that, or at least not until he reached eighteen and put him up against the kitchen wall with the threat that even though he was moving out, he'd return to stab the bastard if he ever did anything to hurt his mother. A tad immature but he couldn't think of anything else to say that wouldn't see him kicking his father to death in front of his mother. She'd stepped between them and begged him to leave before things turned so bad they couldn't be retrieved.

She was a broken woman long before that. There were a lot of broken things in his life – fractured lines in what should have been a healthy, clear path to adulthood. He lifted a clod of mud and dropped it through a gap between the board and the edge of the grave. Maybe it was the noise of the incessant rainfall but he didn't hear what he feared – the sound of dirt hitting wood – his mother's coffin bearing the impact of this open wound.

But then he knew in himself the truth fifteen years had hidden. He knew, as anyone knows, that after such time there would be little left, and the council diggers would've left a layer of clay between her remains and whatever was to be inserted that day.

He had to hold his breath hard to prevent a howl ripping from his chest. His beautiful mother, a wasted woman in the end, driven to despair and into the arms of cancer from the constant stress of living under the regime of such a tyrant. A man who everyone saw as the perfect gent – a real charmer – always smiling and chatting, until he got home.

But he always ensured his girls were out at their clubs and didn't witness his behaviour. Or if they did, he'd explain it all away with the news that their lovely mother had hit the bottle a little too hard that day and he was only trying to prevent her from harming herself or making a show of the family.

Barry took the pink rose from the plastic bag, hunkered down – rain pouring from each rib of his brolly – and remembered the last moments he'd spent with his mother. She'd been gone for days, in a coma after an unsuccessful operation to cut a massive tumour from her womb. He'd held her hand and watched her last breath leave her mouth – a gentle whisper to the universe – the immediate aftermath shattered by his father's anguished cries, his guilt dragging him down so fast he suspected the man was going to keel over there and then in a greedy race to beat his mother to wherever she was headed.

As soon as the funeral ended, Barry turned away and never laid eyes on the man again. Then, fifteen years later, his eldest sister, Monica, phoned to relay the news that their father had suffered a catastrophic stroke that had basically left him at death's door. She'd asked if he wanted to visit before the end.

He politely declined but did ask where the man would be buried, knowing the answer before she responded. The prospect of what was to happen burned so deep into his heart that he couldn't bring himself to share the news with his partner. Instead, he took a leaf out of his father's book and told her some work had come up which he couldn't ignore, and he'd need to be away for a few days.

She'd been fine about it. Sinéad was a good woman but it was obvious she knew something was up. He'd booked a hotel in Dublin and borrowed one of their umbrellas that morning. And now he hunkered at his mother's soon-to-be-defiled grave, a pink rose in his hand, tears raining down his face.

His sisters had pleaded with him to attend the services, for their mother's sake, but he knew it was a ruse to prevent people talking. Let them talk. It was way beyond time everyone knew the truth about the monster. But who would talk about an old man? Because that's what he'd become before his stroke. He'd outlived his wife by fifteen years, and in that time he drank himself into a fat, bloated mess, his baggage pulling him into the gutter of regret. The darkness within had festered and fermented into a poisonous guilt-driven pus that spread through him until he became a prisoner in his own home and mind, uncommunicative in his paranoia, the fear that his wife was haunting him turning him into a creature of the shadows.

Barry shut those thoughts down and slipped the rose through the gap. He wouldn't return. How could he? He would have to find another way. Maybe he'd visit her favourite church. Light a candle and sit for a quiet few minutes. Or he could sit on bench in the park where she liked to walk. Yes, that might do it. He tapped the plywood board once and straightened, shook water from his shoes, and walked away.

Eileen

Mary Minnock

The pain woke Maria early in the morning while it was still dark. The day had finally come. She lay in bed looking up at the ceiling, tensing herself for the onslaught of each new contraction. It was strange and wonderful to think how, later that day, there would be a new person in their lives. Philip lay sleeping beside her and she soaked in the detail of his already well-studied face. Sleep had loosened it, clearing his features, like a blackboard wiped free of the scribblings of the day. His breathing was deep and even, and he stirred as she snuggled in closer underneath his arm. She felt like the luckiest person in the world.

After a while, she shook him awake and told him it was time to make their way to the hospital. It was New Year's Day. The streets were eerily quiet but the hospital was as busy as any other day. Babies didn't know it was a holiday. They were greeted by a cheerful nurse who brought them through to an examination room and asked Maria to sit up on the trolley. She chattered away about the mountains of nappies and baby food the first baby of the year had won earlier that day.

"It's a shame – you missed it by a few hours," she said as she bustled around the room, connecting Maria to the various machines that would monitor the progress of her labour. At one point, her smile skipped a step and Maria's heart quickened. She imagined that the woman forced the smile back on her lips when she noticed her face was being scrutinised. Conversation became a little stilted and false. It bothered Maria and she glanced at Philip to see how he was reacting. He looked concerned but normally so. She tried to shake away her doubts.

The nurse rolled the mobile scan unit away. "I can't seem to get this working properly," she said. "I think we should go to the scan room. The equipment there is more reliable." She made a quick phone call before leading them through the corridors of the hospital to a room where a doctor was waiting. She looked tired and serious.

Wasting no time with formalities, the doctor asked her to lie on the examining table. She squeezed a blob of cold gel onto the mound of Maria's stomach and spread it around with the scanning device. Like magic, it traversed the barriers of her body, showing them her baby curled up in that too-small space, as she had seen her so many times before. Quickly, too quickly, the doctor put the device down.

She took a deep breath. "I'm afraid I can't detect any heartbeat."

Maria had difficulty hearing through a buzzing noise in her ears. Her first thought was: What kind of a doctor is she? You'd think being able to hear a heart beating would be a minimum requirement for a doctor.

She was annoyed with her but decided to remain polite.

"Are you sure?" Philip asked, by Maria's side.

The doctor ignored him and focused her attention on Maria.

"If I wasn't absolutely sure, I wouldn't have said anything."

Each word was enunciated slowly and distinctly, calculated to be a blow to bludgeon Hope to death. But Hope was like one of those monsters – a beast from a Hollywood movie – surging back, bloody and gory, again and again after the audience is convinced that, this time for sure, it has been killed, savagely and without mercy.

The world receded and noises became strangely distant, yet accentuated. She heard them say it was time to transfer her to the delivery ward. Her body felt strange and heavy, as if it didn't belong to her. Her head moved in slow motion and it was like a conversation was going on between two strangers inside. One kept shouting 'No! No! No!' in a slightly hysterical way, and the other one, far more sensible, was calmly saying that this could all be sorted out, that this was a hospital, that things like this didn't happen in hospitals, and that this was just a misunderstanding that would be rectified.

Her labour pains became excruciating, and she was glad. The midwife explained that they couldn't give her an epidural in these conditions. Maria didn't bother to tell her she didn't care. The pain was welcome: it felt right that something like this should hurt this much and, anyway, it gave her something else to focus on. For hours, the contractions lapped over her, becoming more acute and frequent. She felt as though the bottom half of her body was trying to disconnect itself from the top half. If only she could disconnect her brain.

At some point, she started to feel afraid. The fingers of fear reached into her heart and squeezed it. She felt terribly cold. A corpse inside her body was forcing its way out, violently and painfully, a fact she tried to ignore, but she had no choice but to face up to it, and it shocked her. What would happen when it came out? Would it live in her nightmares forever? Would it always throw its shadow over her life?

As labour progressed, Hope made another attempt to assert itself.

"Maybe they got it wrong," Hope, the second voice in her head, said. "Maybe this was just one big mistake?"

"There's no mistake," the other voice said, trying once again to murder Hope. "They are too sure of themselves. They are not allowing for any doubt."

"But maybe..." Hope said, refusing to be crushed.

Through the pain, which had become entrenched now and was starting to feel permanent, they asked lots of questions that she couldn’t answer: how she felt, if the pain was getting worse, if it would help if she changed position, if she was ready to push, if she wanted an autopsy. But there was only one of the questions that seemed to matter, and the answer was obvious without thinking about it:

"Would you like to see your baby when she is born? Do you want to hold her?"

"Yes."

There was no other possible answer but she wished there was. She didn’t want to look at her but she couldn’t bear to not see her. Just as the baby was almost out, while she shuddered through the final effort of expulsion, Hope, mangled and battered, reappeared, showing its bloody head one last time. It tried to convince her that the midwife would shout out in surprise: "This baby is alive. Quickly, help me. She’s breathing." And then they would all move into a flurry of action like on television, doing cardiac massage, connecting machines and shouting for more help.

But this wasn’t what happened. Instead, they stood around her, grave and silent, while one of the nurses wrapped a blanket around the baby and placed her on her stomach. This time, Hope was decapitated, with no chance of coming back. They left the room so she could be alone with her.

She was surprised when she looked down that the baby wasn’t the monstrosity she had been expecting – she was just a tiny baby with pale skin, long dark eyelashes resting against soft cheeks, and a sweet, perfect mouth that would never cry or be kissed. Maria looked down at this small, beautiful thing and she didn’t feel torn apart like she thought she would. There was no violence. Quietly, her heart split open and sadness poured out.

"I’m so sorry," she wanted to tell her baby. "I should have protected you and I didn’t. You never even got a start."

Philip couldn't look at her. He stayed away near the window, gazing at the world outside.

Maria decided to call her Eileen. All of the considerations they had previously taken into account for inclusion in the short list of names were no longer relevant. She no longer had to worry about people having trouble pronouncing it. It would never get shortened to anything else. Nobody would ever use her name to make fun of her in the playground. No one would ever ask her how to spell it. No teacher would ever add the initial of her surname to distinguish her from the other little girls with the same name in the class. Maria suspected she might be the only one to use it, and Eileen was a good name for her.

After about half an hour, they came back into the room to take her baby away from her. There were some complications. Some of the placenta had remained inside. They told her they would need to make sure it was all gone and this might be painful for a while. She didn't care – this physical pain distracted her.

Once it was all over, they wheeled her into a private room. She soon realised that, for a while, the hospital would be divided into two types of people. There would be one type, like the cleaning lady, who looked deep into her eyes and clucked in sympathy at her while she swept the floor. She paused in her efforts to encourage Maria to drink up her tea, as though it were an elixir. Others, in their discomfort and helplessness, scurried past her, avoiding any form of eye contact, as if they were afraid it could reflect the pain and hurt back to them.

After she got home, when the pain regressed and she was no longer numb from shock, she noticed the tidal wave of depression. It was as if she could look over her shoulder and see it there, towering over her, ready to crash down and destroy her. She had to keep running as fast as she could to avoid being whipped up by it and dragged along in its momentum before it suffocated and destroyed her, throwing her away like a rag doll.

For the first months, she felt as if she were running with gut-wrenching speed over long distances, only barely managing to keep ahead of the wave, although whenever she tired or slowed down, she could feel its spray. She ran, believing it was only a question of time before that wave of sadness overwhelmed her, but she kept going, not sure why she bothered. Maybe it was animal reflex – habit. She ran until one day she felt that she didn't need to run so hard. The wave had subsided and it didn't have the power to destroy her anymore. Eventually, she was able to sit down and rest, and the wave only splashed over her feet.

The Sun Is Not At The Table

Eileen Moynihan

Gretchen looked out from the kitchen window and observed that the sun didn't stretch as far as the cemented area in the backyard where the table and chairs stood. They were in the shadow now of the shed and the fence between her and her neighbours on the left. Fading, golden sunlight still danced in the far corner of the garden, where the empty bench had been placed on the bit of lawn to catch any lasting rays. The roses that climbed the fence in that last sunny spot were withering and dropping their petals. Memories flooded her mind, bringing an overwhelming feeling of melancholy and loss.

Only weeks ago, she and Albert had sat at that table in the full heat of an unusually long hot spell. They had moaned about the heat, but at the same time relished the warmth on their bodies, and, the feeling of being 'somewhere abroad' – a sense of relaxation you only got on holiday. It was their little domain and they spent as much time as they could in it. They read, chatted, ate and drank wine or, cups of tea or coffee, enjoyed music on the radio, and listened in silence to the sounds of nature, broken intermittently by the cry of a child or a rumble of a tractor. At night, they lay close together until their perspiring bodies had to part and they threw off the bed-clothes and savoured a slight breeze wafting over them from the open window.

She and Albert clicked the minute they'd met, which strangely enough was at her husband Ben's funeral. He had approached her at the graveside when the crowd were gone and just family milled about, and introduced himself as an old school friend of Ben's. As he shook her hand on that wintry day, a strong warmth seeped into her frozen flesh. She had looked up and, in spite of her grief, was taken aback by how handsome he was. His eyes were kind, his smile sympathetic and she'd smiled back. Then, remembering she was meant to be a grieving widow, she lowered her gaze. She politely invited him back to the hotel for refreshments for family and close friends.

At the hotel she was busy with family and funeral guests but every now and then found herself glancing at Albert. She knew it wasn't right but found herself compelled. While she had loved Ben in her own way, and she knew deep down he'd loved her, too, their relationship had become stale, boring and routine, – a duty. Neither of them had acknowledged it, with each seeking their own space within the marriage, and tolerating their time together. She wondered if Ben's family could see through her. For one reason or another, they hadn't had children. This broke her heart, though she never let it show. Neither of them pursued any medical reasons for their barrenness, and overtime it was accepted between them and was never discussed.

A week after the funeral, someone knocked at the door. When she opened it, she found Albert standing there with a bunch of flowers.

"I just wanted to see how you are," he said, and pushed the flowers towards her.

"Thank you. Please come in." She held the door open, aware of her face burning. "Come into the kitchen. I'll place these in water and put on the kettle. Would you like tea or coffee?"

He followed her in. "Tea would be lovely, thank you."

They spoke about the weather, the garden, his time at school with Ben, her former job as a secretary, and his former job as a local newspaper editor. Time flew, and at one stage she realised she was talking animatedly to this complete stranger.

"I'm sorry," he said out of the blue, after looking up at the kitchen clock. "I've taken up too much of your time. Please excuse me. I don't want to overstay my welcome."

"I enjoyed it," she'd said, sorry he was leaving.

"Well, maybe we could meet up again at the park or something next week? We don't want your neighbours talking." He scanned her face, as if to check whether he'd gone too far.

"I would like that. Ten a.m. next Wednesday, at the bandstand in the park?"

"I'll look forward to it," he said, then left.

After a month or so, they were meeting up several times a week and then most days. One afternoon, they were having coffee and cream cakes in town, laughing about some silly joke, when she happened to look up and saw Ben's older sister Lillian staring at them through the window. Lillian caught her eye, glared for a second, and walked on. Gretchen's face went cold and Albert asked her what was wrong. She explained about Lillian and told him how they had never really got on, as the woman was self-opinionated and snobbish.

He went pale as he glanced out the window.

"Are you okay, Albert?"

He coughed into his hand and smiled. "Ah, that Lillian one. She was always making snide comments about my darned jumpers and patched trousers. Indeed, she hated it when I came round to their house to play with Ben. Ben's younger sister, Muriel, was sweet though."

"Yes, Muriel is lovely," Gretchen agreed.

"Don't mind Lillian. I think it's about time we should be open about being a couple. Time is too short at our age. I think Ben would be glad you have found some happiness. We got on great at school but he changed as he got older, I don't know why. People will soon move on and start talking about someone else."

Gretchen was nervous about being so open about her relationship with Albert but found that most people were genuinely happy for her. Albert had been patient and hadn't made any sexual advances towards her, even though she could sense he wanted to. Of course, they had kissed and hugged and held hands but hadn't crossed the final line. As she began to trust him and miss him when she wasn't with him, she made the initial move one night after a few drinks in the pub. It didn't take much to persuade Albert to follow her lead, and it turned into the most passionate night of her life.

"Let's move in together," he'd whispered in the early light of dawn. I can't live without you." She kissed him in reply and that is what they did. They moved into his place and made a beautiful life together.

For five years, they lived every day to the best of their ability, enjoying one another's company and never taking each other for granted. Muriel often called to them but Lillian never darkened their doorstep. Gretchen had never been so happy or felt so alive. Their love was passionate, tender, and companionable. Then one sunny day at the end of August, Albert collapsed in the garden. He literally had just gone to smell the roses and she'd found him lying on the grass by the garden bench.

She had been inconsolable and never felt so alone or empty. It wasn't the same when she'd lost Ben. On the day of Albert's funeral, Muriel stood by her and guided her along in the blur of the whole event. Lillian sent a card but never came.

Now, as she looked out at the garden, she thought to herself; *the sun is not at the table.* Indeed, for her, the sun would never be at the table again. The doorbell rang, rousing her from her reverie and, with reluctance, she went to answer it.

She found a younger version of Albert standing there. He introduced himself as Harry, and told her he was looking for his father, Albert, and had she heard of his mother, Lillian? After she recovered from the initial shock, he told her he'd been adopted as a baby and had just got up the courage to start looking for his birth parents after his adoptive parents had passed away. She made him a cup of tea and broke the news as gently as she could that Albert had died. The poor chap was impacted, so she tried to help by telling him where to find Lillian.

When he went to Lillian, she shut the door in his face, so he returned to Gretchen who made him more tea and soothed his pained heart over a good chat. Over time, she became like another mother to him, and the sun did return to the table in the garden, and new memories were made.

Memories

Bernadette O'Reilly

Trapped inside a memory
Of best forgotten dreams,
That tear apart one's sanity,
And rip away the seams Of hurt,
That is not yet healed enough
To make a fresh, clean start,
To hide away the loneliness
That makes the days so dark,
So that is why it's best to start
A diary of the heart.

Heartbreak Ridge

Mary M. Trant

The year 1940 was drawing to a close and, for a number of weeks beforehand, my grandmother's heart was continuously pounding and beating like a drum in her chest.

Mum often recalled how her mother sat next to the open-hearth fire in her thatched cottage with a black shawl draped over her shoulders and her hair tied back in a bun – knitting in the hope that this relaxing exercise would cause the irregularity in her heart to calm down.

However, as the weeks went on, the pounding worsened. My mum clearly remembered that a visit to my grandmother's doctor indicated that she was suffering from anxiety and panic attacks.

My Aunt Maisy, Mum's older and only sister, had plans to go to the USA that were at an advanced stage. She was emigrating there to better herself in life, as there was little or no opportunity for work available in her hometown, between the mountains and the sea in County Kerry, Ireland. Helped by a distant relative, she had already found work as a trainee nurse in San Francisco.

A few weeks later, my aunt rode away from the mountains, streams, and the family that raised her, and went to America at the tender age of eighteen. Mum told me many stories about her and how she left, with an old brown suitcase on the carrier of her rattly old black bike.

Before she left, her mother, my kind-hearted grandmother Margaret, sprinkled her with holy water to bless her for her journey. Tearfully, she handed Maisy a small, weathered tin box that contained rubber patches, sandpaper, rubber solution, and a tyre lever – a puncture repair kit – for fear she may hit a pothole or uneven bump on the road and get a flat tyre. Not only that but, regardless of how she felt physically and mentally, she strode along beside Aunt Maisy to a stone-built bridge that stood proud a half mile away. Water flowed under it from the heathery mountains above, and silvery currents danced over smooth stones as the stream made its way towards the sea.

It was here that my grandmother waved Maisy a final and heart-broken goodbye as she watched her eldest daughter disappear over the bridge, wondering whether she would ever see her again. Overwhelmed by sadness, my gran collapsed into tears, unable to contain a flood of emotions. Despair washed over her as she struggled to make sense of it all. Luckily, a neighbour was nearby and came to her assistance.

Crossing the bridge had a finality to it in this lonesome and beautiful place. Just like Aunt Maisy, many young people were wished a sorrowful and heart-breaking goodbye as, like her, they emigrated to foreign lands. Hence the reason the bridge was known locally as "Heartbreak Bridge".

Maisy cycled ten miles to a relative's house, where she stayed overnight.

At dawn the next morning, she cycled another five miles to the nearest train station. After she reached the dim, smoky building, she left her bike in storage, to be collected by the same relations whenever they happened to be in the town.

Aunt Maisy took a train from there to Cobh, in County Cork, and began a long journey by ship to America. Their first port of call was Liverpool – her first time in England – where a huge crowd of people came on board, most of whom were also seeking a new life in America.

It was in the depths of November, with a major storm out in the Atlantic Ocean. The captain of the ship navigated his way around the worst of it, which meant an extra day was added to an already long and arduous journey.

A few weeks later, Mum received a letter from Aunt Maisy. She said that her journey on her bicycle to the train station was not a pleasant one, as it was raining and cold, but she assured Mum that her train journey to Cobh was reasonably good.

Aunt Maisy said that, even though the journey by ship from Cobh to the USA was lengthy, and despite the weather conditions, she met some nice people onboard. Some had brought their old button accordions and flutes with them, and they had merriment, singing, and dancing, managing to keep their spirits high throughout the journey. She mentioned the mouth watering food they enjoyed aboard the ship and said she had never in her entire life tasted sustenance so good.

Over the coming years, she studied hard and became a nurse but, because of her continuing studies and busy nursing career, she never got an opportunity to meet the man of her dreams, so remained single.

She missed Mum and my grandmother dreadfully. Mum often shed a tear when she spoke of how far away her sister lived, and their only communication was the letters they exchanged. When I was born, Aunt Maisy sent me beautiful clothes regularly and, in her letters, always asked Mum to give Maggie hugs and kisses from her Aunt Maisy.

Shortly after Mum received her first letter from her sister, my grandmother suffered a stroke, due to cardiovascular disease, and went to her eternal reward. Mum often spoke of her sadness at the loss of her mother, and the fact that Aunt Maisy could not make it home for her funeral was agonising for both of them.

In my latter childhood days, I passed over Heartbreak Bridge on umpteen occasions with Mum, and it was a stark reminder tome of my grandmother's heartbreak when my Aunt Maisy emigrated to America.

Bog Trippin'

Alec Secam

Dr. Byrne haloed his finger around the base of the large screen, as if digging his hand into the murky depths of the Bog of Allen itself. A pensive frown rippled across his forehead.

"I know it's a lot to take in, a lot to swallow, but these scans reveal a lifeform visible here in the central aspect of the bog, pulsating approximately five kilometres below the crust. Its core is as large as your average house. That's the area of concern."

He wiped perspiration from his brow. With his tired, gravelly voice, he'd outlined the living organism's prognosis multiple times already. From top-level brass to today's working group. And the pushback at every level of the scientific institute had been exhausting. Now, more than ever, he needed people to listen. To realise the true danger festering below the surface of their average, boring lives. To awaken them to the dark destruction this organism could unleash on the whole Island of Ireland.

"The organism is *essentially* the 'memory' of our country. The living memory of Ireland. These veins, or arteries, run for kilometres up through the peat bogland. Like all things living on this planet, it feeds on oxygen and mineral properties, which it wrenches from the ancient bog – a source of superfood nourishment. Like all healthy memories, it functions to help the island decide its future, learn from its past, and know right from wrong. It is highly complex and intuitive. A key part of our ecology and evolution.

"And now the crux of the problem. This fog, or shadow, which is cast across the central aspect of the scan? That is a progressive disease fuelling the deterioration of Irish society. The disease is blocking vessels in this clouded core, preventing the essential flow of oxygen and minerals, and releasing deadly emissions instead. The lack of empathy, the uncontrollable greed, the soaring homicide rates? All are caused by the rapid decline of the memory. Putting it simply, this invasive fog is a form of ruthless dementia, attacking the core organism and stifling the memory. The impacts are visible for us all to see here above ground."

***

Siobhain's heart skipped, and butterflies fluttered in her belly. She looked around the small meeting room. Her colleagues' faces shifted in puzzled bewilderment. A few light gasps. Faint muttering. Furtive glances. An electric energy flowed through the room. Her fingers turned ghostly white as she gripped her notebook, her head dizzy in the wake of Dr Byrne's damning revelation.

"To conclude, we have been tasked as a matter of urgent national security with clearing this infectious cloud at the core of the memory. We must stop this creeping dementia before the entire country is lost to chaos and violence."

The fluorescent lights and sterile surroundings of the modern meeting room made the story told by Dr Byrne seem unreal, akin to a science-fiction tale rather than a pressing scientific mission. It made some sense, Siobhain thought, as she contemplated the vacant world she had come to inhabit in her middle-age. Fear of attack every time she left the house. Crippling debt for the simple pleasure of living. The absolute lonely wreck of the last decade of her life. Yes, it made perfect sense. Perfect crackpot sense. Dementia. Why not?

She scanned the nonplussed faces around the table. Dr Watts caught her eye. He sat smug, flanked by impressionable juniors, confidently stroking a trio of expensive-looking silver rings on his left hand. His wide grin mocked the daunting task laid out before the small team of scientists.

"Is this some kind of joke, Doctor Byrne?" he asked. "This elaborate tale was entertaining. I'll grant you that. But, really? We have important projects already close to deadline. And now this dementia farce?"

"Well, Doctor Watts, this is what we have been put here to do. Today, it's science for the greater good. Everything else stops. This project, and the health of the memory organism under the Bog of Allen, is all that concerns us now."

Dr Byrne's voice balanced coolly on the brink of impatience as he dragged his hand through a dishevelled mop of black hair. His stern eyes held firm on each member of the small scientific team. The coarse response dissipated any clouds of doubt in the room.

"To state the obvious, our country is on the brink of collapse. We have traced the decline directly back to toxic emissions seeping from the Bog of Allen. We must fix this before it ruins us all. We have to go down there. We have to neutralise the infection. And we have to do it straight away. Team members best suited for the job will be selected in the coming hours."

***

The Monarch, a silver bullet-shaped capsule, looked wholly alien as it moved through the natural wilderness. Inside, Siobain took temporary ease in the passing colours of dried turf piles and explorative butterflies. The vast bog stretched for miles around, with a blanket of purple gorse and waves of green rushes as far as the eye could see – the flora and fauna that attracted her to life here in the first place. All tranquil and serene.

"Well, Doctor Watts, I can't say I expected us to be paired together for this one. But here we are."

Her voice shuddered, and she checked her safety straps again. She tapped the monitor in front of her, and it sprang from standby to life.

"We're making history, Siobhain. Real history. And call me Daniel, please. I was sceptical at first, when Doctor Byrne bumbled and babbled his way through the details. But this trip, this memory thing under the Bog of Allen? Well, the more I thought about it, the more I realised it truly is a once-in-a-lifetime opportunity. What harm can a little bit of fame do, right?"

A wide smile broke across his chiselled face, the man already wallowing in the fruits of his future fantasy.

"Well, Daniel, it's just another whacky story in the newsfeed of life for most people. You know yourself. People will scan the headline, pause a second, and move on, right? I agree, if we don't fix this, it will result in a growing hell for everyone. But, at the same time, I wouldn't expect a mob of fans and cameras to greet us when we return above ground."

***

Daniel dismissed her rapid reduction of his vision. He slapped on the Monarch's sweeping strobe lights as they moved below the bog's crust and deeper into the unknown of the tunnel. The strong beams blasted away the darkness ahead, revealing surrounding walls of sogging black peat. Brown water dripped from all parts of the artery's porous sponge-like surface. As he checked the monitors for crucial oxygen and location readings, he couldn't help but wonder if they would feature on the evening news. Could they be headhunted by generous-paying Scientific Institutions? Or even make the history books? Surely, he figured. Restoring order and peace to a society on the brink? Definitely.

***

Siobhain watched with trepidation as they travelled deeper into the cave-like artery. Its surface grew drier, until it became obvious they were no longer in a bog tunnel, but inside the alien anatomy of the memory itself. She marvelled at the unnatural wonders on display. They were arriving in a new, unfamiliar world. The soggy peat walls had given way to a more crystalline, permanent bright-blue resin. It calmed her, taking the edge off her earlier crushing anxiety. The ceiling of the artery had become smooth, now showing a glamorous pattern mix of white and pink. Dashing, vibrant streaks. Sharp blue veins cut through the irresistible shades. The colours jumped wantonly at her retinas and, as she sat there, she found the whole cavern alluring and seductive.

Daniel shifted in his seat, his gaze darting conspicuously across the oncoming array of unfamiliar textures and unnatural candy colours. He continued his nervous boastful chatter. No doubt, Siobhain reckoned, to play down the otherworldly, alien nature of these new surroundings. His face was sweaty, his hands clawing as he scrolled through the vehicle settings on the monitor. I bet he wasn't expecting it to be like this.

"Check out the veins woven into the artery ceiling above us, Daniel. What do you suppose those hazy liquid pulsations are zipping through them? They sure flow real quick. Some form of nutrient?"

"It could be the noxious emissions Doctor Byrne was rabbiting on about? Either way, I don't like it. These surroundings, this whole vein thing – it isn't natural, Siobhain. We are over halfway to the core now. Not far from the infected area. In fact, I would say this whole organism is an infected area, but I'm not the boss, unfortunately. I'll prepare the canisters. Better to be ready."

Siobhain remained silent as he released his safety harness and proceeded towards two metal canisters secured at the back of the Monarch. Each canister was knee-high and filled with a specially prepared chemical mix – the antidote to the noxious emissions wreaking havoc across the island. She leaned out and watched him check the spray pressure and tug the backstraps on each. He didn't have to say it, but she was sure all he wanted to do now was reach their destination, apply the chemical mix, and get the hell back above ground as soon as possible.

They continued to autopilot through the blue-crystal cavern. Siobhain studied the surroundings with an unfathomable appetite. A blue so endearing and inviting – she had never seen anything like it before. So peaceful, so beautiful. A new world. Adrenaline surged through her body.

"All ready for application, Siobhain? Won't be long now."

Daniel strapped himself back into the seat and tapped the monitor for a location update.

"The government should think about building more prisons, if you ask me. Violent criminal gangs can't be helped, Siobhain. Certainly not by us spraying some pesticides into the Bog of Allen. They are only going to offend and reoffend. This whole operation is ridiculous, really."

He rambled on, delegating plans to rid the world of his dislikes. Siobhain almost shook her head with disgust. Has he even opened his eyes to where we are? This beauty, this new discovery, this real-life miracle?

She held onto her harness as they rumbled over rougher ground. Specs of dust and particles spattered the wide front window. Rain? Surely not. Within seconds, it had grown to a full torrent, with heavy showers of loose matter pummelling the Monarch. An underground storm, and the vehicle shook under the onslaught, the violent drift blinding the whole view outside the Monarch.

Daniel's protesting voice faded in the background, and all Siobhain could hear was a faint scream. It became increasingly audible through the speakers around them. A mild anguish grew to an all-encompassing howl, and she grimaced at the agony dripping from every soundwave. Like a trapped beast screaming for mercy. Sorrow swelled like an ocean within her, and she feared her world was caving in as a drowning dark presence engulfed her, overwhelming her as she sat strapped in her seat. When she turned to Daniel for an explanation, all she saw was a cowering man, his head hunched as he shivered over the monitor.

"Stop the Monarch *now*, Daniel!"

He held his head, as if the howling was beating through it, his mind clearly a flood of confusion. But he must have heard her because he scrambled for the settings on the monitor before dragging the cursor downwards with shaking hands, slowing the Monarch to an eventual stall. He blinked several times, his struggle obvious as he tried to focus on what was visible outside. The storm was receding, and they had come to a stop in a wide oval cavern.

"Daniel, let's get this done, yea? It's all getting a bit weird. I think we know we're not wanted, right?"

They strapped the canisters to their backs and held the sprayers at the ready, both masked up as they exited the Monarch's slide door. Siobhain felt the bounce at once under her feet – the strange softness of the memory vein surface. All was still outside. Then Daniel stumbled forward, clumsily expelling a mist of chemical antidote around him.

A moment later, both of them stopped in their tracks at the sight ahead. A striking blue female form, with arms outstretched, merged into the wall, frozen in crystalline grace, as if on a premade altar. Mysterious formations were sculpted into the blue resin all around her. Proud cryptic testimonies of a new existence beyond their comprehension. The figure looked with yearning through long wavy hair at both scientists. A feed of vivid blue veins ran from every angle of the artery into her torso – blue shots of life flowing with urgency to keep her aloft – in power. In control.

"She's alive, Siobhain. She's scanning us right now. You see? The responsiveness in her eyes? That's...amazing, quite frankly."

They both stood in awe at the blue woman woven into the cavern wall, like a crucifixion frozen in time.

"Yes, it looks like she is in fact alive," Siobhain said. "Fascinating. Should we take some kind of...samples? This must be the origin of the organism. Isn't she beautiful?" She stepped closer to the altar, unable to refuse the sudden irresistible draw.

Is must have been the same for Daniel, because he moved up beside her, standing face to face with the figure. Her large globe eyes peered longingly into his, probably into his very soul, and his features softened, as if all the fear within him had dissipated. Then her mouth opened wide, her jaw strong, and her lips clutched at the skin on his neck. Daniel stood there, helpless under her control, feeding her graciously, until his body fell limp.

Her elegant hand reached out to Siobhain. Subtle smooth fingers, offering peace, calm, eternity – all the things she was missing these past few years. All she wanted for the years ahead. As the jaw slickly closed around her neck, she felt life itself surge through her like a bolt, lifting her into the air, her feet becoming a lightning rod of energy. Her eyes fizzled as she took in the majestic pink and white ceiling above. Soon, she would be part of this wonderful new world of memory.

Zoe's Birthday Party

Roisin Coyne

My memory relates to writing about Zoe's sixteenth birthday party.

I could say it is simply just happy or sad, but I would prefer to call it bittersweet.

You might be wondering why when most birthday parties are supposed to be happy.

Not to spoil it too much, but I would feel bitter sweet if pixies started to argue over where the crown should go on a cake.

What is the big deal, pixies?

It's no big deal, that's for sure!

Or if a sugar-obsessed unicorn just couldn't wait to get her hooves on the Princess's birthday cake!.

But one thing I wouldn't mind is the Lion of Wisdom warning me about the mysterious dark unicorn terrorizing the people of Tropiganza.

And that's my piece of memories

Thank you for reading.

The Light Between Us

Joanne Ryan Curran

I'm in Grace's nursery and she's crying again. Not just crying, she's screaming, and it's piercing my mind. I want it to stop. Her face is getting redder and redder with each scream, and she's pounding her little fist against the wooden rail of her cot.

"Please, please stop, Grace," I shout at her. "Please be a good girl for Mammy."

She screams louder. I sit on the floor and drag my knees into my chest, noticing the stains on my top from spilt milk. I painstakingly chose this top this morning to make myself look normal, but I don't look normal. Far from it.

I should pick her up and feed her, but I can't face it. I just don't have the energy. I wish I was more like the old me. I miss the old me. What's wrong with me? I remember the old me. The one that was capable. Who knew what she was doing. Before I went on maternity leave, I was a manager, and people came to me for answers to solve their problems, but I don't feel like that person anymore. That version of me has left the building. She checked out long ago. Motherhood is not turning out the way I wanted it to. I can't even manage my own child.

The curtains are drawn, and the nightlight is still on, even though it's eleven a.m. I don't have the energy to pull open the curtains and turn off the light. The room is perfectly decorated in pink, with a pastel-coloured mural of baby animals on the wall, and shelves filled with muslin blankets and teddies. Her fairy bunny and giant giraffe won't stop staring at me. No one told me it would be like this. That you could love someone so much it hurts, and at the same time you forget who you are. I can smell her organic lotions. There's nothing like that scent. I remember buying all this stuff and feeling confident at the time that I would provide her with everything she needed.

She would never need for anything.

"Make it stop,' I scream. 'Somebody make this stop."

But no one replies.

My hands are shaking as I make the call.

Why is Mam's phone ringing out again?

I'll try my sister, Mary. She'll know what to do. Mary will be there for me. I can depend on her.

She answers. Thank God for that.

Her voice is edged with concern. I know she's worried about me. She probably thinks I have post-natal depression. But I don't. That's not it at all. I just have too much to do.

"Calm down, Fiona. You're not making much sense," I hear her say, but in my head, I'm making perfect sense. Why doesn't she understand me?

"Take deep breaths," she says. "It's okay."

"She won't stop crying, Mary. I just want Grace to stop crying. I need to get away from here."

'She's probably just hungry. Just feed her and stay on the line. You got this, sis. I won't leave you.'

I pick Grace up and feed her while my tears drip onto her precious face. The poor child. None of this is her fault. She deserves to have a mother who knows what she's doing – who has her act together. My mind is racing with thoughts of how bad a mother I am. I dry my eyes, knowing I need to calm down before James gets home from work. I bet all his colleagues' wives can mind their children just fine. I can't let him know how I'm really coping.

Once Grace is fed, she stops crying. My little girl is happy again. I burp her and she gives me a big smile. I try to smile back, but it offers her no comfort, and she cries again. I think my

"I'm going to come and see you," Mary says. "I'll check the flights from London. I'll come as soon as I can get time off work. Is there a local parent and baby group you can join? I'm sure there is."

I had thought of joining one for a bit, but I couldn't face looking at all the perfect parents while I'm struggling.

"Hmm ... I don't think that would be my thing," I reply.

I zone out of our conversation as memories flood my mind of the day Grace was born. The 24th of September and the sun shone in Dublin. It was love at first sight. I couldn't believe she was mine. All mine. She was the most perfect thing I'd ever made, better than anything I've ever accomplished. I was on a high for a few days after her birth, and pretty much all she did was sleep and feed. She was a dream baby.

But after I brought her home from the hospital, it all changed.

It was as if an alien or a strange animal now lived with me. It didn't feel like she was a human being. The experience was like nothing I'd read about in any of the baby books. She didn't have a clue where she was or why she was here.

What I want more than anything is for the crying to stop. Grace is two-and-a-half months old now and there's no way I can keep this up much longer.

More tears well as I think about her in pain. God. I don't want to start crying again.

I zone back into the phone call. Mary says she has to get back to work, so I phone some friends and my two other sisters. They're all busy – with work or just rushing out the door. They all have lives –

busy, important, and successful lives. Everyone knows what they are doing. Except me. All I have now is the memories of who I once was.

The walls in the room are closing in on me, it's as if they'll squeeze the living daylights out of me if I don't get out soon. I grab my coat and handbag and rush out the door.

I run as fast as I can, until I'm out of breath. Once I stop, I remember Grace. I can't believe I left my beautiful girl on her own. Images flood my mind like stills from a horror movie. There's a shadowy character grabbing my girl, and he's going to take her and keep her for his own. In my mind, Grace is screaming, waiting for me to come save her. I shake my head to block out the thoughts. What the hell is wrong with me? Who in their right mind would do that to my child? No one would. So why am I thinking this way?

I race back to the house, half expecting Grace to be gone. Everything is quiet and still when I arrive there. I'm afraid to walk into the nursery. I tiptoe in. Grace is lying on the floor cooing away to herself. My heart soars with relief.

"I'm sorry," I say as I kneel beside her. "I'll never leave you again."

The shrill sound of my phone ringing startles me. I'm afraid to answer it in case I sound odd so I let it ring over and over again. What if they lock me up and I never get to see Grace again? On the fourth call, I realise the caller's not going to give up so I answer it.

"How are you getting on, love?" my mam asks. 'I was out at the shops earlier. I just saw all the missed calls from you.'

"This is really hard, Mam," I whisper.

"I'm on my way," she says after a heavy silence. "Just stay where you are. I remember what it was like."

Mam arrives carrying a bag filled with lots of stuff – a bit like Mary Poppins – and I have no idea what's inside. I just see a strong, capable woman in front of me. She would never get herself into this mess.

"When did you last sleep?" she asks me.

"I haven't," I mutter. "I don't remember the last time."

"Now, go to bed and sleep and I'll look after everything here." She touches my arm. "Grace will be fine. I'll talk to James and fill him in."

I let her take over and the next few days go by in a blur of sleep, where I'm awoken only in darkness to eat and drink. I'm comforted by the darkness, and the pills prescribed by the doctor make me sleepy. At the end of the week, Mam insists I let her open the curtains and allow some light into the room.

"The sun will shine again," she says. "You just can't see it yet."

On Christmas Eve, we walk around the local village. It snowed this morning and everything glistens. We pass the pretty church and the clock tower, then move along and end up at a Christmas market at the village hall. Mam is in her element browsing through the locally made pies, cakes, jams, and Christmas gifts. She buys a few things for our lunch. I find I'm no longer edgy, and I buy some jewellery, along with baby clothes for Grace. We wander down the hill from the market to the bridge at the southern tip of the village. It's where the weavers' cottages, rippling river, and wraparound woodland come together. This is my favourite part of the village, and today I take in all its beauty. We walk back to my house in comfortable silence, with Grace asleep in her buggy.

"Are you tired?" Mam asks as we get in the door. "Why don't you take a rest and I'll get lunch ready. Hopefully she'll sleep for a bit longer. The colic seems to be easing now."

"Mam, how did you know what to do?" I ask as I take off my coat. "How did you know what I needed?"

Her eyes soften through a short silence. 'I remember those early days with you. One day at a time, pet. That's how I got over it."

She pats my hand and a rush of love fills me, and I feel hopeful for the future. I'm ready to be me again and create new memories.

Watching

Yvonne Brewer

This poem is from "Twigs.", by Yvonne Brewer (2018)

We watched for the school bus.
It was cold, so we stayed inside, sitting on his bed,
as his bedroom window had the best view, and
the bus could be spotted as it made a left turn
at Stack's crossroads.

We watched for the school bus, and he saw a huge bird,
floating in the icy wind over Patch's field.
"It's a hawk!" he shouted.
"He's watching something!"
We watched as it held itself together in the wind.

We watched as it did not take its eye off its target.
We watched as it remained focused,
never letting the weather stop
his wants, or needs, or purpose.
The bus arrived. I watched as he ran onto the bus.

His black coat untied and blowing like bat wings around him,
Moone Boy's cap in his hand, blonde hair blowing, carefree.
"Put on your cap, zip up your jacket," I shouted in my Mum voice,

But he ignored me and climbed onto the bus,
excited after the adventure we just had.

I knew how much he loved feeling the wind blowing
around him, and was probably imagining he was
the hawk, or a bigger bird.
I watched the bus drive off.
I let the wind carry my whispering prayer.

To always keep his wings strong. To keep his spirit soaring.
To keep his eyes focused on what's important. To always remember
that life can pass by watching buses, or life can pass by watching hawks,
watching something. Being who they are. Living their dream.
Letting the wind bend their wings, but not shake them from their true path.

Galway

Val Robus

As I was walking down to the village this morning, I got the smell of a turf fire. It took me right back to my school holidays, which were often spent visiting my granny in Galway. Those visits were a real culture shock to me. Home was a busy town in the UK, where there was always something happening, and there certainly weren't any open fires where I lived. We just flicked a switch, and the gas boiler came alive.

Even though my granny lived in Galway City, it was like going back in time; the pace of life was slower, and everyone knew everyone else. I would hop on my bike and cycle for miles, along country lanes bordered by stone walls, with grass growing in the middle of the road. I'd marvel at the statues of Mary and Bernadette that I'd see in the many shrines along the way.

I remember the sun shining. It probably wasn't always that way, but that's what I remember. I used to be sent to Danny's huckster shop for the messages. That was another difference – it was called shopping in the UK but going for messages in Ireland. Danny had a warm smile and a twinkle in his eye, and his shop had everything. It also saved a trip up the hill to Roches Stores, and he always gave me sweets because I was a visitor. I remember candy sticks, golf balls, and, of course, Tayto crisps.

Quinnsworth was a highlight of my visit. We didn't have Quinnsworth in the UK, and I found it fascinating, especially the make-your-own-pizza section. This was in the 1970s, and I'd never seen anything quite like it. I also loved the roller disco near the GPO. I loved it! Hours of wheeling around to the latest songs, and not having to listen to the bickering that was going on in the house at Woodquay.

I spent a lot of time outside, mainly because my mum and dad were always trying to improve Granny's house, which she hated. She liked her outside toilet (even with all the spiders), and didn't want a bath, preferring instead to douse herself with TCP – another smell that still stirs memories, and not in a good way!

There are so many things I could tell you about the renovations! Looking back, it's like something you'd see in a comedy show. My dad was always picking up things at car boot sales. He'd spend the days before loading up the car, and on one occasion the roof rack was piled so high, it took the garage door off as he reversed the car out!

That was a particularly memorable trip. We unhooked the door and went on our merry way, around the winding roads of the Welsh mountains until we reached Holyhead and the ferry terminal. The customs guys decided to search our car – probably because it was packed to the gills. They found white powder in a clear packet and dad was whisked away for interrogation, despite his pleas that it was just wallpaper paste he'd picked up at the boot sale! They realised he was telling the truth after they tasted it! Needless to say, he always bought branded wallpaper paste after that incident.

When we arrived at Granny's house, there was no warm welcome. On most occasions, she'd be over in the Abbey for mass, so we'd have to wait for her to come home. The kettle would be filled and she'd dander about, muttering 'Maw, paw, kettle', and spitting on the range to see if it was hot enough to start dinner.

Dad never wasted any time and would be off with his tools looking for something to fix. One day, as Granny was washing the dishes, he came crashing through the flat roof of the scullery and landed in the sink in front of her. He managed to save the Sacred Heart picture from landing in the water by grabbing it on the way down. The air was blue that day! And funnily enough, it cut our visit short!

My childhood visits to Galway were always so different to my life in the UK. Sometimes, I just wanted to spend school summer holidays at home with my friends, with hot running water and an inside toilet. The cycling and the roller disco made up for it, though, and now that I'm older, I can understand why my granny just wanted her life to be left as she liked it.

Sky Words

Kathryn Crowley

Poetry first moved me as an eleven-year-old in school when a nun recited *'I Wandered Lonely as a Cloud'*. Eyes sparkling, her palms dancing, Sister Assumpta seemed to grow taller for certain stanzas. Her performance was made all the more entertaining whenever miniature comets of spit shot out from the gap between her two front teeth. My friend Siobhán and I would glance at each other, then erupt into giggles. We were never scolded.

Most of the time, I listened to the teacher intently, thrilled to be in the presence of a true artist. I remember how, a few days after electrifying the room with poetry, she asked if we were familiar with the dawn chorus. Thirty-five blank faces stared back.

"Birds. Singing at daybreak," our guide prompted. "Raise your hand ... Anybody?"

She launched into a brief monologue to expound on the beauty of birdsong. For part -two of our lesson, she sketched out a huge uterus to explain the role of sex in reproduction, waving a piece of chalk around as an orchestra conductor would their baton.

Today, I relish listening to a solitary bird at dawn. The chittering begins just as pink rails of magical light appear in the indigo sky. Daybreak. Soon, I hear a warble, then another – squeaky notes and rough caws. It seems that hundreds of voices join in until the whole world becomes a soundscape, and the sound is in me, and the birds are the sky, and we're all pure sunshine, and nothing is separate, and I breathe it in deeply as the waves rumble their bass notes in the distance.

Granted

Eamon O'Leary

Look at the state of the place. And look at the state of him, leaning on the shovel, borrowed no doubt, gawking at the plane playing hide and seek with the clouds. The shirt clinging to his back – that'll be last night's drink trying to escape – he's not what I expected in a son-in-law. The pneumatic drill will be thumping in his head. Serves him right. I've a good mind to yell in his ear hole.

Every weed known to man has found its way to that mountain of topsoil, where I thought he'd have a lawn laid. Legions of nettles, thistles, and dandelions. It's like the word's gone out: – "Come on over, yer man's an eejit."

What would the girls at bridge think if they saw this eyesore?... I hope those bramble tendrils cut the legs off him.

"Morning, Ed, darling. You're at the weeds again, I see."

"Yeah, I'll give them another lash of weed killer later, but I think they're immune to the stuff – I wonder where that's headed. Maybe Majorca, or the Canaries. Jeez, I'd love a holiday. Claire's in the kitchen, ironing a couple of my shirts. I'll have a cuppa with ye."

I'm sure he will. His tongue stuck to his palate, going on about a vacation. As if he's not already away with the fairies.

"Take your time. I baked scones and made raspberry jam for you pair of lovebirds last night. I'll get Claire to stick on the kettle and heat the scones."

"You're a star. Watch your step. The rain soaked those planks."

"I'm used to the obstacle course by now."

Planks. I ask you. Planks are one thing. This is a war- zone more like. March 1980 and the bungalow plonked in the corner of Tommy McCarthy's misshapen acre. The few tons of hardcore dumped where the bulldozer gouged an entrance, swallowed by the muck and long since gone. As is the builder, who scarpered when the money ran out. Rubble everywhere and you'd drown if you fell into one of those trenches, filled with Lord alone knows what. No high heels here. I'm relegated to wellies, trying to get in and out without breaking my neck. Thankfully, there are concrete floors. Imagine the mess if they had carpets?

"Hi, Claire, love. Is it safe to come in?"

"Hi, Mum. Yeah. Ed says he's defeated the last battalion of mice. There was a tiny gap by the sink. He's blocked it and the traps haven't been touched for two days."

"Thank goodness for that."

He'll be acting the hero now. Hunter, gatherer, protector, all that.

"Were ye out last night?"

"Nah, I didn't bother. Ed went for pints with the lads after work and met the rugby guys in the Corner House later. I'm getting my hair done, so we'll probably go out tonight."

"Did you have time to look at curtains? That rug pinned to the bedroom window looks awful from the road."

"I know what I'd love to buy, but the mortgage is crippling us. The interest rate has gone up again. Did you see? Eighteen per cent now? How they expect people to pay that, I don't know. We'd be sleeping and eating off the floor if it wasn't for you, Mum."

Here he comes, puffing and panting like a hound after the chase. At least he's kicked off those manky boots.

"I got the whiff of the scones. Is the brew ready?"

After gulping down the cuppa, Ed applied copious amounts of butter and jam to a second scone, topped the lot with mountains of cream, and scoffed it in one go. Then, with a raspberry streak on his chin, he headed off to scavenge in the hedgerows for firewood. *Firewood! I ask ye. Oh, they have central heating, but no oil, and no money for any either. Eighteen per cent and all that. Thankfully, the sun was giving its first lick of summer, and they won't look like Travellers for much longer lugging barrow loads of kindling.*

Ed came back as I was about to leave, risking life and limb to get to my car.

"Met the postman outside, the usual bundle of begging letters. Have another mug of tea and thanks again for the telly. I got it working with the rabbit's ears."

Claire flicked through cheerless brown-window envelopes and dumped the junk. A flyer announcing direct flights to Athens caught my eye. Then it sounded like there was an explosion in her brain – a wonderful one. Squealing and whooping, words running into one another, she waved an official-looking letter in Ed's face.

"It's here," she said. "It's here. The grant is here."

Ed looked as if someone had plugged him into the mains, jumping and bouncing before the two of them began jiving about the kitchen, their smiles getting wider and wider, like children on Christmas morning.

"Will one of you tell me what's here?"

"Mum, it's the grant. The new house subsidy from the government. A thousand pounds. It's more than I make in three months."

"That's fantastic. I'm thrilled for the pair of you."

Calm restored and after more tea, himself went back to conquer Everest and the weeds. I started a list.

"First thing Monday, I'll get curtain books from Dorothy. I know her from bowls. She'll offer us a good deal. Then, I'll call and pick up wallpaper and paint cards from Colour It Right and give James in Floors Alive a shout. He's expensive, but top quality."

"Thanks, Mum. I'm so excited."

The next few weeks were frenetic. Using a milk crate for a stepladder, we measured. Walls, windows, and floors, length by breadth. Confusion, as my yards, feet and inches clashed with Claire's centimetres and metres. I left the maths to her. In the kitchen, the picnic table I'd given them groaned under tomes of carpet books. I kept fit crossing the gangplank, a volume of wallpaper samples under each arm acting as ballast. We scoured through the lot 'till we were cross-eyed.

With a to-do-list that filled my notebook, a thousand pounds wouldn't go far. It would be tight, but with my connections, they could do the bed and living rooms, tile the kitchen, and maybe carpet the hall. I'd suggested to himself that he might make a start on the paths and that mountain of soil he played with every month. He looked at me as if I'd announced an intention to do a poo.

"Can't do anything too physical 'til the season ends. We're in the County Cup final in three weeks. I can't risk getting injured pulling and dragging stuff around. Anyway, the place is all muck after the rain."

"I see."

Struggling, but showing the patience of Job, I kept my gob shut.

And then – and then – well – the end of the month came, and payday for them both. Claire invited me for dinner on the last Sunday, as per usual. My contribution: a delicate white for both of us, himself would gannet the red, a cheapie Rioja. We had roast beef with all the trimmings, and homemade Yorkshire puddings to boot. And the calorie-crammed eclairs were yummy. A pleasant evening, although I thought the two of them were childishly giddy. We joked at the surreal scene, concrete floor, the wobbly table laden with gourmet food on bone chinaware and finest crystal. They had done well on the wedding presents a year earlier except for the four toasters, three kettles and the regular mantelpiece fodder. Lifting my long-stemmed goblet, I was about to propose a toast to the imminent decorating, but Claire beat me to it.

"Mum, we've news."

I almost choked on the Chablis.

"What? I'm going to be a granny. Oh my God, I can't believe it, but I didn't think you were planning to start so soon."

"No, no, no, Mum. Don't be silly. I'm not preggers. We're going on holiday."

I managed a weak "What?", and despite the wine, my colour drained, and I felt a migraine coming on.

"Two days in Wexford wasn't much of a honeymoon, and Ed says we deserve a holiday. And do you know, Mum, you can fly direct to Athens? Anyway, we've decided to use the grant money to go island hopping in Greece. For three weeks. Would you be able to give us a lift to the airport next Saturday?"

9th May 1981- the details are chiselled in my brain.

And they went. I went to see Dr Murphy. He prescribed a mild sleeping tablet and suggested I cut down on the G&Ts in the evening. The cheek of him. Those junior doctors think they know it all. I reminded him I'd survived a World War and would get over this bombshell.

I gave a few of the walls a lick of emulsion when they were away, but the list went in the bin. Postcards arrived from Paros, Ios, Mykonos and some place that sounded akin to something you'd catch – Sifnos, I think it was. They came home bronzed and broke. I got the obligatory bottle of ouzo, which I used to strip the paint off a bedside locker.

For weeks, Ed first regaled then bored me with tales of their adventures.

"Did I tell you we slept on beaches a few nights?"

"Sounds so romantic." *But no mention of the mosquitoes or other creepy crawlies.*

"Yeah, gazing at the stars makes you think of things – like infinity – even eternity." *Looks as if we've a philosopher in the family now.*

"And the ferries were amazing. They go everywhere... and on time."

Sardined into the petrol-scented bowels of a Greek ship isn't my idea of a holiday.

"And we brought back loads of photos. Getting them developed at the end of the month."

I'd had enough and was ready for home when a beaming Claire added: "And that's not all we brought back."

"What's that?"

"I was going to wait. Y'know, 'till it's safe. Superstition and all that. But I can't. You're going to be a granny. I'm two months gone."

It took me a few seconds to cop on, though her words were plain enough. Then it was me jigging around the kitchen, as happy as a dog with ten tails and all ten wagging.

Back home, I rummaged and found my knitting bag. Took a few days to find my rhythm, but I got going. Cardigans and socks and bunnies and blankets. Maybe it was after staring at the stars, but Ed calmed down a tad when fatherhood loomed. Working at the speed of a drifting iceberg, he made gradual headway before eventually conquering his Everest. He wasn't slow to moan about his aching back and blistered hands, though, the poor wounded hero. Claire, as thin as the garden rake to begin with, did her bit, hauling away bucket after bucket of stone before becoming the self-appointed Minister for Blossoms and Blooms. When finished, it felt as if they'd turned a corner. Some of the mayhem had evaporated. The emerald-green lawn running down to the hawthorn hedgerows gave the house a settled feel.

Susie arrived safe and sound and beautiful. Chaos returned, but it was just the chaos of a child. I spoiled her rotten, of course, but that's what grannies are for.

Masons laid paths, and Ed surprised everyone by building an acceptable low, dry-stone boundary wall. Progress, I thought. But Claire's blood pressure rocketed when he arrived home with the remnants of an ancient school desk.

"You're not bringing that junk in here. Where did you get it?"

"I rescued it from a skip."

In it came, and nights of sanding, varnishing, and cursing saw it restored. I don't know where he got it, but seeing the inkwell, complete with brass lid, brought back memories. As did the blackboard he acquired from God knows where. The walls of the room he'd commandeered were covered with stencils of animals, trees, and a giant rainbow.

"All ready for Susie," he said. "I think she'll be a teacher."

Mission accomplished; they headed off again. A bargain, last-minute cancellation. Where else but Greece? I said nothing but was thrilled. I'd have Susie, who had taken her first steps, all to myself for the week.

It was lovely, that time with Susie. You forget, between your children and your grandchildren, all the fun of having a whole young person to yourself.

And they brought home more good news. "Most people bring home a few bottles of duty-free," I said to them but I was only messing. Linda, the little darling, arrived the following spring.

"Must be something in the water," Ed said.

"More like something in the drink. 'Tis a wonder you didn't call one of the girls, Alexandra or Athena or the like."

"Maybe next time."

"Hold on a sec here," Claire said. "There won't be any next time. Finito. I won't go as far as making you have the snip, but I might just hide your passport."

We laughed, raised our glasses, and offered thanks for our blessings.

Time slips by, especially with two young girls in the house. The far-from-finished house. Rooms are a work-in-progress, one at a time. The bedrooms are painted and carpeted, and undeniably snug, but elsewhere, concrete reigns supreme. In the living room, family photos, a window to times past, fill a wall. My favourite: a grainy image of great-grandparents, Cornelius, ramrod straight in his Sunday best and Nora, forbidding, enthroned alongside in all her finery.

Thankfully, the driveway is finished. The bitter-sweet smell of asphalt lingers on hot days. I like the contrast with the earthy cow-dung aroma from McCarthy's nosy cattle who peer over the wall.

We're doing a barbecue this evening, and I'm in charge of the salads. While picking lettuce, radishes, and spring onions from the raised bed, I peek in at the girls in the playroom. Susie is busy squiggling shapes on the blackboard. Her friends, arms folded, legs crossed, cosy up on the floor, while a menagerie of teddies sit at the desk waiting for class to begin. Linda is busying herself crawling through an obstacle course of toys.

Ed arrives back after cutting my grass and hedge, and fixes me a house-measure G&T. He cooks the obligatory sausages for starters, then he's off like the Pied Piper, the children in tow, frolicking about, smiles as wide and bright as the sun, queueing up for spins in his wheelbarrow. The girls chattering is as loud as the cluster of blackbirds in the whitethorn, while the boys concentrate on the scabs on their knees. It's intoxicating, infectious, and perfect. Perfect, except for that plane thundering overhead. The kitchen windows rattle in protest.

"C'mon, Gran," Susie says," let's play aeroplanes."

And so, here I am, arms outstretched, soaring, swooping, and laughing.

"Where's that one going, Gran?"

"Haven't a clue, love. Perhaps Majorca or the Canaries, or even Athens."

Looking skywards, I wonder if anyone on board is as irresponsible and daft as my pair were.

Grandfather's Clock

Niall O'Connor

Elvis, the Monkees and Jesus,
all superstars in my younger years,
now demystified
by the miracle of an ordinary life.
But still the tick of my grandfather's clock
closes itself around my heart each night,
echoing through the moonlit landings,
calling until there is no choice
but to be borne along by its clinical beat;
time sliced neatly and laid down
frame by frame,
memory by memory,
like a butcher peels rashers from a grunt deceased,
a life laid bare, and as yet not fully told,
re-dreaming a lost and pointless vision
of what was never to be.
I place my hand
in the way of the scythe-singing blade,
vainly trying to put a stop to its sway,
crying out, that what is written,
and yet to be written, coexist
in the same passing stream.

I question
whether it is stillness
or movement
that serves reality's illusion best?

Leaving Home

Tom Moloney

I looked around my bedroom. Thanks to Mam, the place was tidier than I'd seen it all summer – everything in place, even the bed, dressed for when I'd return for the Halloween break. She was more likely to do surprises like that whenever something was on her mind. Like the time she kept me at home from school because I was sweating, coughing, even raving when sleeping. She lit the open fire and brought me toast and scrambled egg. A special breakfast. And as soon as I was finished, she closed the window blinds again and tucked me up, then whispered to me to try to sleep and I wouldn't have any school 'til I was well again.

She had obviously tidied my room in the afternoon while I'd gone out to say goodbye to *Shot* and *Magoo.* They lived in a kennel in the backyard. When I returned, I could get the aroma of baking in the kitchen.

-Smells good, Mam.

She smiled, obviously pleased that her baking wasn't being wasted on the kitchen air.

-I just had a mind to bake some queen cakes before you go. And you can bring some with you. A snack for later in the week. You never know, you might be feeling hungry. She then said: And don't be disappearing too far now. Evening tea will be ready before you know it.

Nobody said too much at teatime. I ate four of the queen cakes. Dad ignored them, sticking to his usual boiled egg and soda bread. As for Mam, she placed one queen on her plate but, as I remember, didn't actually eat it, just sipped her tea in between fidgeting with the tea cosy, making sure it was covering the teapot correctly. She also moved the sugar bowl, marginally. On doing so, the jug of milk had to be adjusted. Eventually, she stopped and asked me if I'd told the two dogs that I'd be home at Halloween. And then she asked Dad if there was enough petrol in the car.

-Everything is hunky dory, thanks to our young man. He reminded me as we passed the *Lobitos* pumps on the way home from Billy-the-barber. Whereupon he reached for another slice of Mam's soda bread and, as he began buttering it, gave me a nod and a wink.

After tea, it was time to dress in my room for the journey. As I did so, I thought of the moment earlier when I waved goodbye to *Shot* and *Magoo,* the two of them wagging their tails as if nothing was up, not the least concerned that when I'd see them again, the long nights of winter would be well and truly *in situ.*

I gave my reflection in the wardrobe mirror a final look over. A strange vision, to see myself fully dressed in the boarding school rigout. Awkward even. Maybe the self-conscious age I was at added to the moment, complicated by the tight haircut from Billy-the-barber earlier that morning. That kind of cut was alright when I was eight or nine. It meant I could go for longer without another one. But I was only months short of my thirteenth birthday and, even though my hair was blond, there were moments during the summer when I day-dreamed of leaving it grow, long enough and shaped in the style of Georgie Best. And yet, I didn't feel brave enough to let Dad know of such a radical plan. He hadn't moved with the times when it came to hairstyles, and the same could definitely be said of Billy-the-barber.

When my turn came that morning, I succumbed in silence to the status quo. Billy asked the predictable: Will I take much off?

In those days, boys were seen, not heard.

Dad said: You'd better give him a good bare one. I don't know what arrangements they have where he's going to. Maybe none. A lot of hair could grow before he's home again. And his mother mightn't recognize him. Who knows, they mightn't even have any barber.

Billy began shearing as he said: Even though the city is probably full of barbers. Amused at what he'd just said, he added: Of course, that's neither here nor there if the boys are all locked up.

I'd say Billy took pleasure making me look like a twelve-year-old Kojak. And in between humming away an oul' song about taking him back to the *Black Hills,* himself and Dad agreed it was a pleasant day for the beginning of September, although the summer overall was disappointing and September was already showing the same pattern. When he had finished cutting, he asked: How's that? You'd pass for the army now, not to mind boarding school. I stroked the few hairs he'd left on my head, putting on a defeated glance in Dad's direction as I left the swivel chair.

On seeing my image in the bedroom mirror, I imagined that if I walked around the village, the locals would be staring at me, wondering if I was the same person they always knew. The smell of newness from my blazer, along with its crisp feel and gold buttons, exaggerated the strangeness about this new me. I left my bedroom and tentatively took the few steps to the kitchen.

By the time I was ready, the village church was pealing out the Angelus. Mam and Dad didn't delay in dressing and were waiting in the kitchen, Mam no doubt reciting the Angelus to herself, having long given up on him joining in when it came to moments like that.

Maybe Dad copped that I was uneasy on entering the kitchen. As I stood there with a sheepish grin, he smiled and, nodding to Mam, said:

Well, well, if our little boy hasn't turned into a dapper young man in his college outfit. Not only is he smart, as I've always said, but now he looks it as well.

That was the first time Dad had seen me in my college rigout. Mam, however, had taken me to Limerick city in mid-August to Todds. She knew from the college prospectus that they were the official suppliers of blazers and slacks for boarding school. And so she already knew how I looked in my new attire. Which meant she wasn't as carried away when I entered the kitchen. But she agreed with Dad: You're absolutely right. Then, focussing on my tie, she said: Hang on, your tie, slightly crooked, and beckoned me to come closer so she could adjust it to her satisfaction.

-I think that's better. Her straightening of my tie, I sensed, was more in the way of an excuse to delay the final moments.

Mam's mothering was soon interrupted as Dad said: Shush, is that rain? He lifted the window lace and looked out. Sure enough, the pleasant evening was after changing.

-For once, the forecast is right, he said. God, I hate driving in that stuff. And the dark along with it. And the blinding lights, to boot, and those goddamn wet streets. He then felt his pocket for the car keys. Half-reassured, he said: So, are we all ready?

Mam didn't answer but, as she put her finger in the Knock font, said: Wait! And she sprinkled holy water. Dad hedged his bet and blessed himself, along with me and Mam. For whatever reason, there was nothing more to say. Dad opened the hall door. The rain greeted us.

The Ford Anglia was parked beside a puddle of water. Mam scurried close behind me, spotting the puddle at the last second. Careful, she said. The puddle, your pants.

I negotiated the puddle and settled into the back seat, my new navy blazer with the blue and red crest of my impending Alma Mater, matching grey pants and navy tie, none the worse. And my feet were getting used to the feel of a new pair of black shoes. They were my first pair of slip-ons and I'd taken them from their box only fifteen minutes earlier.

Mam had put on lipstick and make-up, and under her overcoat was wearing a navy dress with white buttons. A pink hat that seemed to be tied to her hair with a pin at the back covered her head. I was sitting behind Dad's seat. From there, I could see Mam's profile. She was in fidgeting mode again, soon finding a chamois cloth in the glove compartment. She began wiping the front window.

The car itself was cold. It might explain why the scent of whatever perfume she was wearing consumed the air.

Dad was also dressed in his Sunday best. He glanced at Mam, putting back the chamois cloth in the glove compartment and switching to fidgeting in her handbag. As she held a Kleenex to her eyes, he refrained from saying anything. Instead, he leaned over his shoulder and, without being able to actually see me, said: Everything ok back there, buddy?

-All ready.

Would my journey have been the same if, just as Dad put the key in the ignition, somebody in our village with the gift of premonition had run towards the car, waving her hands and shouting: Stop, I've something to tell the child, something I think he should know.

Maybe it was just as well all those years ago that a would-be clairvoyant never appeared out of nowhere almost breathless, tipping at the window inside which I was sitting, gesturing for me to pull it down, ignoring my parents, as if what she had to say was for my ears only. And in all that time, too, maybe she continued to stare like one transfixed, in possession of a great secret from the omniscient spirit of the universe.

As I'd half-roll down my window, she'd confide: I think you have a right to know that you are leaving home, *forever.* She'd hesitate after saying *forever,* as if guilty at having to tell something so final to a child, at the same time relieved that she got the chance at that pivotal moment in my life to tell me to my face the truth of things: that as soon as the Anglia left the yard, there would be no turning back.

Not knowing any better, I'd look upon her as crazy but I'd say thanks in order to get her away from my window and might perhaps have the temerity to suggest she go home out of the rain. I might even smile, and her gaze would soften to one of pathos for the way things happen in life, and then she'd despair that what she'd just told me was being drowned in the rain and the dark.

As Dad would begin steering the car towards the crossroads, already on alert to the bleakness of the journey before him, me sitting in the back seat, no longer really visible to the would-be clairvoyant, who knows, she might very well shout: Innocent little boy, I'll light a candle for you!

O'Malley's Ghost

Robert McDermott

Whoever said there was solace in age was a fool, O'Malley thinks as he trudges down the stairs at five in the morning. He's pushing seventy and the years sit heavy in his bones, like thick snow on wispy birches. His clothes are neat and respectable, a vestige from his father who impressed upon him that clothes maketh the man. O'Malley wears a necktie every day and clips it to his shirt with a modest tiepin. His thinning hair is combed across his scalp and the smell of pomade hangs softly on the air in his wake. He has scrubbed his nails and applied a cedarwood aftershave balm, a Christmas gift from his daughter. This is not vanity. The balm protects his skin from the elements.

Once downstairs, he doesn't take breakfast, never eating before noon. He fills a glass from the tap and drinks half of it. The rest is poured into the cat's bowl. O'Malley never knows where the cat is except that it's somewhere, usually lurking in the shadows. Entertaining a wistful thought, he puts kibble in its food bowl, dons his cloth cap, and steps into the bracing air of late February.

The yard sits in the hard dark of night. It's too early for the meridian of dawn to bisect the horizon. Brighter mornings will be here soon enough, O'Malley thinks, but for now he must endure the dark. Rising early doesn't bother him, it also maketh the man - no, it's the darkness that eats at him. He walks to the Land Rover and checks he has everything. Lambing season is busy, and Dwyer is expecting him. After that, Riordan. Both have good-sized flocks with robust ewes. O'Malley doesn't anticipate any complications, but something unexpected always comes, and whatever it is, he's ready. A thought about the calving finished earlier in the month surfaces in his mind. It was a hard year. Some years are uneventful, and some are not, he supposes. He doesn't dwell upon it. Birth and death are a routine and unsentimental aspect of his duties.

His wife died ten years ago. She wasn't yet sixty and lingered for over a year. Unable to do anything about it, O'Malley carried on during the day and spent the evenings sitting with her, recalling better times when the girls were young, and the summers were dusted with soft yellow light well into the evening. Memory is invincible, his wife would say, it's even stronger than death. Her courage humbled him, and her good humour, even in the face of the inevitable, kept both buoyant. But for all this, it was her gratitude which astounded him. How she would tell him she had a good life and no regrets and how she'd made him promise to adopt an attitude of gratitude once she was gone. Now, in the dark before dawn, he thinks of her, says her name aloud and tells her he is grateful for the day to come, a ritual he has performed every morning for a decade.

He opens the driver's door to get into the Land Rover. Venus, sparkling in the east, catches his eye. He pauses for a moment to enjoy its familiar presence, and thinks how the stars, despite the vast distance of space, appear so near when the sky is clear he could reach out and touch them. He shakes the wistfulness from his head, puts his leg into the car, and is about to let the seat take his weight when he hears something behind him. He's tensely balanced half in and half out of the car, waiting for another noise. When he hears a footfall on the gravel he steps from the car and turns around. Accustomed to the dark he discerns the shape of a good-sized man. He waits for the man to speak.

"Howya, boss," says the man.

O'Malley feels blood rise in his face and the heat of it stuns him.

"There's nothing for you here," says O'Malley.

"No bother, boss."

Even though O'Malley can't see the man's face, he stares at him.

"I was going to knock in on you, boss, thought you might have some work. I could take a look at the shingles on that building over there."

"I said there's nothing for you."

After a long silence, the man claps once, loudly, and takes his leave. O'Malley watches him move off towards the road, waits a few minutes, then goes to the building the man noted. He gives the lock a hard tug before opening it and entering. The sharp resinous smell of creosote and decades of accumulated assortments hits him. He turns on the pale light and surveys the area, locates what he seeks, retrieves it and leaves. After extinguishing the light, he bolts the door, goes to the Land Rover, and gets in.

As he drives out of the yard, phosphorescent flecks of dawn crack through in lines of rose and gold along the cobalt sky. The emerging day reassures O'Malley. About half a kilometre down the road, he sees the man strolling along slouched-shouldered and swag-bellied. His hands are so deep in his pockets, it's as if he's trying to scratch an itch on the surface of his knees. His head is bowed, and O'Malley passes at a slow pace. The man doesn't lift his head, preferring instead to salute him with a flick of his cap. O'Malley maintains a slow pace while looking into the rearview mirror. He expects the man to turn around, or at least stop, but he never does, and O'Malley, satisfied for now, continues.

Later, after his rounds, O'Malley is at home where his eldest daughter Aideen is making tea. Though she would never say it, she finds making tea on the stove a nuisance. She bought her father an electric kettle soon after her mother died, but he wouldn't have anything to do with it. He never gave a reason. It's now in the shed with all the other things he has no use for.

"Did you go to Riordan's today, Daddy?"

"I did."

"Any bother?"

"Not this time," he says.

The kettle whistles and Aideen lifts it off the ring. The teapot is ready, and she pours the boiled water into it, then takes it to the table. O'Malley watches her intently.

"They had a hard time at the start of the year. How many calves did they lose?"

"Four, and a good cow."

"It's not easy, is it?" Aideen says.

O'Malley nibbles on a crust of bread. Aideen makes him a loaf of brown bread every other day. It's her mother's recipe. O'Malley thinks it's decent, though he'd never say as much. Once the tea is poured a deeper quiet settles between them. He takes a sip of tea.

"Nothing like a cup of tea," says Aideen.

The banal pleasantries continue until O'Malley's reticence finally breaks Aideen's sense of propriety.

'What's wrong with you, Daddy? You've had a face like thunder since I arrived.'

O'Malley is halfway through his tea before he speaks.

"One of the tinkers from Tinnock Hill was here this morning."

"I don't think you can call them tinkers, Daddy,' she says. '*Travellers* is the proper term, I believe."

O'Malley's eyes grow wide, and he mutters something under his breath.

"What happened?" Aideen says, after a moment.

"I was on my way out. He was standing there in the dark with his eye on the shed."

"The one with all Mammy's stuff in it?"

"What other one is there?" he says gruffly.

"You're sure he was a Traveller?"

"Don't be foolish,' spits O'Malley, his patience finally worn through, 'I've been here long enough to know who's who."

"Of course, Daddy," says Aideen.

Their eyes lock and the silence returns, and after a moment, they settle back into it. O'Malley finishes his tea and bread, and soon enough he signals that it's time for Aideen to leave.

"Would you like Colm to drop by in the morning? He could keep an eye on the place while you're out and about."

O'Malley shakes his head.

"What about the guards?"

O'Malley's face hardens.

"The guards won't do anything. Sure aren't they afraid of them? No, there's nothing to be doing until they come back."

"They?"

"The fellow who dropped by this morning was there to size me up. Tomorrow, he'll come back with others, but I'll be ready."

"I think it's best if you go to the guards, Daddy."

O'Malley smirks knowingly. Aideen's eyes flash with concern, but she has no agency when it comes to her father's affairs.

"You don't need to be worrying about me, you don't live as long as I have without learning a few tricks."

He closes the door before she can object, then goes into the kitchen and puts on the radio. He usually prefers the sound of a voice, but now he turns it to *Lyric FM*, takes a seat and allows his thoughts to wander. During a Schubert quintet, the cat appears from the dark, curls around O'Malley's leg, and disappears once more.

The next morning, O'Malley rises just before five. He's in no hurry, he knows they'll be there. By the time he gets to the hallway, the first light of dawn is flaring. He looks at the rifle he took from the shed the previous morning. It's old but in perfect working order. He bought it years before in the event he had to shoot an animal in distress. Using it to protect his home had never crossed his mind, until now. He places a cartridge in the slot, snaps it into the gun with a sharp click, and steps outside where they are waiting for him.

They have come in a van, intending to take what they can. The van's headlights glare into O'Malley's face but he resists the urge to shield his eyes. He doesn't speak and moves purposefully towards the shed. He takes out his keys and unlocks the door. The light from the van casts a pale arc and he can see the gathering, backlit as they are by the dawn. There are six, maybe seven. Even in the thin light, he can see their startled eyes. He notices that none of them carry anything. They are restless, and jabber in low voices like hyenas.

"Story there, boss."

The man from the morning before emerges from behind his men. His fat gut protrudes from between his shirt and trousers like a grotesque eye. He carries a hurl.

"I told you there's nothing here for you," O'Malley says.

The man opens his arms and looks back at his horde.

"We'll decide what's here for us, boss."

O'Malley raises the gun. The younger men twitch. Their jabbering gets louder.

"Don't be foolish, boss. No sense in anyone getting hurt."

O'Malley steps forward. The man holds his position, but his band take a step back.

"You'll not go in there," says O'Malley, his voice shaky in the morning chill.

At a nod from the man, the horde forms a semicircle, closing in on O'Malley. He doesn't know where to point the gun and, in the end, realising he's beaten, lowers the gun and stands aside.

"That's reasonable of you, boss," says the man.

"There's nothing in there," says O'Malley. "Nothing of use to you. Just things belonging to my late wife."

The man smiles. His face is fat and greasy, his lips thick, and his teeth broad. He leans the hurl on his instep.

"No need to lie to us, boss. Sure, if there's nothing in there worth having you wouldn't be standing there pointing a gun at us."

"They're my memories," whispers O'Malley, "you can't have them."

The man snorts and opens the door to the shed. The horde gathers around the doorway.

"I wouldn't go in there," says O'Malley.

Something in the timbre of his voice makes the intruder pay attention.

"What's that, boss?"

O'Malley looks into the man's eyes, watching as they flicker around, unsteady and uncertain.

"I've seen my wife's ghost in there many a time. When she died, I couldn't bear to have her things in the house, so I put them in there. I suppose she's still attached to them. If you take her things, I'm sure she will follow you."

The man laughs, but it's a cracked laugh. His horde shifts on their feet, and O'Malley can sense they're poised, ready to run.

"You didn't say anything about a ghost," says one of the horde.

"I'm not going to take anything from a ghost," says another, "it'll come back on me."

The man looks at his men, opening his arms as if to placate them. O'Malley knows the balance of power has shifted. The man then looks at O'Malley, and O'Malley sees his eyes are alive with fear.

"Go in if you must, but whatever becomes of you is not my doing," he says.

The man sucks in his lower lip and steps into the dark. He's no more than six steps into the shed when a shadow moves across his line of sight, and something crashes onto the floor. The man yelps and bolts out of the shed with remarkable speed for such a corpulent body. His boys follow, and within seconds they've all barrelled into the van and screeched out of the yard in a wail of wheels and smoke.

The smoky odour of rubber fills the air, and O'Malley allows himself a wry smile. He steps into the shed and turns on the light. The cat is sitting there before him, licking its paws. O'Malley reaches down and rubs its muzzle. The cat purrs contentedly and follows him into the yard and towards the house. O'Malley looks towards Venus, thinks about his wife, thanks her, and steps inside.

The Happiness Clinic

Camilla Galbiati

My husband is dead.

These four words float around my head, chasing each other, stuck like a broken record.

My husband is dead.

I won't hear his voice, his laughter, or see his smile again. I won't feel the soft touch of his fingers on my bare skin or the warmth of his embrace. I won't kiss his lips anymore; those lips that made me fall in love with him in an instant. He is gone. In his place, he has left a hole, a void which shall never be filled.

I wander aimlessly through the house. His belongings are everywhere as if, overnight, our home had transformed into a museum in his memory. His black coat hanging by the door, a scarf tucked in its sleeve. His collection of old records neatly arranged by the vintage radio. A guitar abandoned in a corner of the sitting room, a red pick stuck between two strings. For a moment, I imagine him sitting on the sofa, scruffy hair, unshaven, wearing his favourite red hoodie, plucking away at his guitar, humming a tune he has just conjured up from nothing.

Overwhelmed, I run to the bathroom, but, even here, I cannot escape the signs of his presence. His blue toothbrush is beside mine in the holder by the sink. The square mirror is still decorated with splashes of toothpaste. It used to drive me crazy, but he joked that it was like having our own Pollock painting. When he said that, I wanted to strangle him; now, I think I will never wipe the glass again. I open the cabinet and, inside, among the array of make-up items, creams and perfumes, I find a bottle of his favourite after-shave. I instinctively grab it and spray it copiously on my neck. It is like being enveloped in one of his hugs. For a few seconds it is comforting. Then, my heart breaks all over again.

Tears streaming down my face, his scent mingling with mine, I rush to the bedroom. There is a glass on his bedside table. It is half-full, the mark of his lips on its rim. The new Ken Follett novel is beside it, a receipt sticking out of its cream-coloured pages. He never used bookmarks; he found them superfluous. Beside it, some Nurofen tablets, a box of tissues and his mobile phone. The Gardaí found it a few metres from the scene of the accident. It won't turn on. The screen is shattered into a thousand pieces, just like my heart.

I slide my hand in the pocket of my dressing gown, take out my phone, drop on the bed and open WhatsApp. I know I shouldn't do it. It will only make it worse, but I can't help it. Perhaps self-torture is all part of the grieving process. I scroll through the dozens of messages of condolence, ignoring them, until I find his name, a red heart emoji beside it.

Leaving work now. Love u. xxx. His last words to me.

My reply is short: *I made cottage pie, your favourite. Love u xxx.*

He never got to eat it. It is still in the fridge. I couldn't throw it out. As if keeping that mix of mince, peas, onions, and mashed potatoes will bring him back to me. What a ridiculous idea! But there is no right way to deal with grief, is there?

I discard the phone, close my eyes and let my hands slide over the sheets, imagining I'm stroking his naked body. I picture my fingers raking his dark hair, slowly lowering to his nape, then crawling down the length of his spine. I think I can feel his breath tickling my cheek and I turn to kiss him. When I open my eyes, of course, he is not there.

There is no one, nothing. No husband, no marriage, no growing old together, no love, no happiness. Just grief, overwhelming grief.

I wrap my arms around my chest as if I can keep my heart from shattering into pieces. Memories of our life together flash before my eyes. Our wedding day, black suit, white dress, beaming smiles. Evenings spent on the sofa, watching our favourite TV programmes, my head on his chest, his arm resting on my back. Nights in bed, falling asleep in each other's arms. The rows, usually about something silly, unimportant. The walks on the beach, the Saturdays with friends at the local pub, the holidays together in charming sun-kissed places, the laughs, the tears, the kisses...

How can I be expected to look to the future when I seem to be stuck in the past? There must be a way to learn how to live without him, how to deal with grief.

I sit up, dry my tears, take a deep breath, feel my body relax. Then, I outstretch an arm and instinctively grab my laptop from my bedside table. I open the browser. The two O of 'Google' stare back at me, like a pair of round eyes, judging me, waiting for my next move. I sigh, rub my hands over my eyes, then type into the search bar 'how to deal with grief.'

I get thousands of results. Articles, blog posts, even videos. I select an article titled 'The 10 steps to deal with grief' and start reading it. The information is general, with no original methods of coping with grief and no magic solution to erase the pain. The message is simple. It's written in capital letters, highlighted in red, halfway through the article: 'Take time to grieve.'

I don't want to wait. I want a quick fix. I want the sadness to go away and the pain to stop. I shout in frustration, my anger directed at the author of the article, a certain Mary-something, experienced grief counsellor. I'm about to throw my laptop across the bedroom when I notice an ad, in the bottom right corner. It is simple: a black background, a woman crying, and the words 'Tired of grieving? We can help!'

Without hesitating, I click on it. It redirects me to a website. At the top, in bright orange letters, a simple title: 'THE HAPPINESS CLINIC'. Below, a brief explanation. 'Experiencing depression? Have you lost someone dear? Struggling with grief? We are here to help you. Our experts at the "Happiness clinic" will make you smile again in a matter of seconds! Make an appointment here.'

I don't even question it. I need help. I need a quick fix. I click on it. They have an appointment available for tomorrow at their clinic in Galway. Perfect. I select it, put in my details, pay the deposit. I immediately receive a confirmation text. I close my laptop, inhale deeply, then slowly exhale. Soon, very soon, I'll be happy again.

***

I stare at the building in front of me. A modern two-storey, grey structure with small windows and large automatic glass doors. It doesn't really scream happiness. I take out my phone and read the message again. The address is correct, I'm in the right place. The plaque at the door confirms it. A griefless life is only a few steps away, literally. I tighten my scarf, straighten my hat, and walk towards the doors. They slide open, welcoming me like an open-armed mother.

The interior is bright and extremely white. White floors, white walls, white ceilings, white LED lights. I freeze for a moment, unsure what to do, where to go. Then, I notice a desk at the far side of the entrance area. I head towards it. A girl - silky blonde hair, manicured hands, slender body, professional outfit - is sitting at the desk, going through some papers. She raises her head and offers me a perfect smile as I approach.

"Good afternoon. Welcome to The Happiness Clinic. My name is Angel. How may I help you today?"

For a second, I stare at the receptionist, open-mouthed, enchanted by her melodious voice. '*Is she even real?*' Then, I manage to stir from the torpor-like state and answer, "My name is Niamh O'Connor. I have an appointment."

"Let's have a look," she responds, turning her head towards the large screen on her desk and speed-typing on the keyboard. "Oh yes, here you are. Niamh, four p.m. The doctor will be with you very shortly. Take a seat in our waiting area."

She points at a bunch of white leather armchairs neatly arranged around a white coffee table. I thank her with a nod and lower myself onto one of them. It is very soft, comfortable. I'm so tired, so sleep-deprived that I could just close my eyes and—

"Niamh?"

Startled, I open my eyes. A woman is standing before me. She is stunning, top-model stunning. Tall, really tall, with a mane of glossy auburn curls flowing down her back and a pair of light-green eyes. An immaculate white doctor's coat clings perfectly to her toned figure. She smiles and I feel my body relax. I don't know this woman, but I trust her, completely trust her. This goddess of happiness is going to help me, I have no doubt.

"Come with me," she says, beckoning me as she swivels around. I get up and follow her down a short corridor. She holds open the door of Consultation Room D, and with a simple gesture of her hand invites me to step inside. I obey. It is small and quite bare. Just a desk, two chairs, a couple of filing cabinets, and a small plant in the corner.

"Please, take a seat."

I comply and watch her do the same.

"I'm Doctor Hannah," she says, arms elegantly resting on her lap. I can't help staring at her lips as she speaks. I admire their plumpness, their shape, and the shade of her lipstick. "So, tell me, Niamh, what brings you to The Happiness Clinic today?"

There's a lump in my throat. I force myself to swallow.

"My husband... He..."

I'm struggling to find the words.

"Your husband?" she prompts me in her honey-like tone.

I hesitate, afraid that voicing what happened would make it real; but, I realise, it is real, it did happen.

I shut my eyes and finally blurt out, "My husband is dead."

Dr. Hannah looks at me intensely but remains silent.

So, I continue. "He died over a week ago in a horrific car crash. The other driver was drunk, speeding."

"That's terrible. I'm very sorry."

"I've been finding dealing with grief really hard. I miss him, and the memories of our life together haunt me. They are everywhere. In our house, in town... I don't want to be in pain anymore, I don't want to..."

Tears are coursing down my cheeks. There's no stopping them.

Dr. Hannah hands me a box of tissues. I take one and dab my face with it.

"Don't worry, Niamh. We can help you find your happiness again."

A strange sound, something between a cry and a whimper, escapes my lips.

"You will be happy. The process is easier than you may think."

She opens a drawer, looks inside it, and takes out a colourful brochure. She slides it towards me. I pick it up and study it through my tears. The first page is taken up entire by the clinic's logo and name. Inside there is a picture of a woman sitting in an armchair, a strange helmet on her head, two doctors at her side holding iPads.

"Our team of talented researchers have developed a new technology which allows us to enter a patient's mind, through a completely painless procedure, and erase memories of a person."

I stare at her, dumbfounded.

"People from everywhere have visited our clinic in the last year. Some of them have asked to forget about the bully that taunted them at school or the partner that abused them both mentally and physically. In many cases, just like you, patients have asked us to delete memories of a deceased spouse."

My gaze flickers from the woman on the brochure to the one before me. My mind is spinning as I try to understand the meaning of her words.

"The procedure costs nine-hundred euros. All you have to do is sign this...' She reaches towards a pile of neatly stacked papers, grabs one and slides it towards me. '... consent form in which you declare that you've asked us to erase all memories of... just write your husband's name here."

She taps an empty space on the form beside the phrase 'person the patient wishes to forget' with a pen and then hands it to me.

My fingers are trembling, but I manage to wrap them around it and scribble my husband's name.

"Wonderful. All you have to do now is sign it and we can start the procedure immediately."

I lower the pen to the paper. The thumping of my heart is deafening. I hesitate.

"Will you erase all memories of my husband?"

"Yes, Niamh. You won't remember anything about him. It will be as if he never existed."

I look into her green eyes for a moment. Then, I slowly move my gaze to the form. One signature, one simple procedure.

Happiness is what everyone dreams about, what everyone seeks, desires. If I do this, I will be happy again. No more sadness, no more grief, no more crying myself to sleep, no more yearning for my husband. At what cost, though? We are not just flesh and bones. Our memories are as much part of us as our organs, our cells, our bones. They are what defines us, what makes us unique.

"I can't do this," I exclaim, dropping the pen on the desk and standing up. I walk to the door and open it.

'Niamh, wait!' Dr. Hannah calls after me. "Don't you want to be happy?"

My hand resting on the door handle, I turn around and stare at her.

"I want to be happy, and I'm sure that I will, one day, but my husband was the most important person for me. I loved him. I still do. I don't want to lose the memories of our life together, no matter how painful remembering can be. Goodbye, Doctor Hannah."

My final words still echoing through the consultation room, I shut the door and walk away.

The Deepness Of The Brave

Orla McConnon Bakerberg

Note from the author: Written for our late mother, whose soul was taken from us on Sunday, 13th September, 2015. My father's heart was broken, and he left us on Friday, 25th December, that same year. He never missed a Christmas with Mom, even after 54 years together.

The braveness of kind,
A mother of love,
A lifetime of memories,
She now loves from above.
A woman of strength,
For her, giving was key,
A nurturing soul, an adventurous heart,
Overcoming adversity, for her, was an art.
To rise, to live, to breathe, is what we do each day,
For some, that is not always the order, for some, it is still our way.
The deepness of the soul,
Brave,
Strong,
True,
The openness of the man,
How we so miss you.
Life's adversities, overcome,
Loving from deep within,

Affection, hard to show,
Where did it all begin?
Adventurous to the core,
Along a road, windy and long,
Strength and belief throughout,
As you seek where you belong.
Dreams of hope, as they come true,
Always believing in those around you.
A world of love, created,
A lifetime of hopeful plans,
Lay firmly in your hands.
We follow in your footsteps,
We dream your dreams of hope,
You left your strength with us,
As we live and learn to cope.
Pass on the love, the braveness, and all that is kind,
In our parents' love, is where all these we find.
In the presence of a Robin,
Within the softness of a feather,
You are always near me, as I hold your hearts forever.

Leading Lady

Mary Egan Campbell

I watch John as he makes his way down the path towards me, his pace slow. But I am invisible to him. He is oblivious to all but the once-glorious picture house at the other side of the town square, a building which, for decades now, has stood idle, unloved and forgotten. Four score and ten years to the day, he has a surprising spring in his step and a straightness to his back unseen in men half his age. Something I have always admired in him. But then, most men were better built in his day, just like everything else.

On his arm hangs an old overcoat, threadbare now, just like everything else he owns, and a plastic shopping bag, which is meant to save the planet, and comes in handy for carrying all his bits and bobs.

Today, like most Tuesdays, it contains gardening accoutrements and an old bathroom spray-cleaner bottle filled with washing-up liquid and water. It's for the roses. He says it keeps the green-fly away.

At the intricate front portico, he stops and looks up, straining to see out from under his trademark peaked cap, the front of which seems more of a flap now than a peak, drooping with age, just like himself. To the onlooker, he seems to be watching the upper windows. Waiting. For what, who knows? Perhaps he expects a face to appear there - a memory of a happier time. He always smiles as he gazes up. A look so warm it crinkles around his eyes and reddens his cheeks.

Methodically, he sets about laying out his equipment on the ground, spread out across his old overcoat in precise order. Once this task is complete, he gets to work. With increasing difficulty, John lowers his stiff frame to his knees, then rests back on his boot heels for a moment to take a breath, before launching into his ministrations. It's the same routine every time, come rain or shine. He tends to the little patch of roses he planted in the grassy area to the side of the front steps, sheltered from the weather in a south-facing sun trap, where they have thrived and delighted all passers-by for decades. The roses, at least, are his, although by now I'm pretty sure he has squatter's rights on the tiny garden plot he has commandeered too. Besides, the town council are only too happy to let him maintain and brighten up the place. As a result, he has been minding those plants with all the care and love of a new parent, for nigh on sixty years now.

They were her favourite blooms, this her favourite place, and the little garden has long since become his shrine to her.

When the movie theatre closed its doors for the last time fifty-seven years earlier, it seemed to everyone who cared to notice that a part of John wilted and died along with it. The Silver Palace was his last connection to her. His strongest most vivid memories of her were created on that spot. The place where they first met.

And how do I know all these things? Well, I was there too.

As a young lad, John was taken out of school to work with his father cleaning windows. Though not old, his father no longer had the legs for climbing. Besides, he could use someone strong to steady the ladders, so John, being the youngest and the biggest of his brood, got the job. He was initiated into the family business without ceremony or consultation - a bit like being drafted into the army - so that was that. You never questioned why. Not in those days. John, being an outdoorsy sort and not so fond of the books to begin with, was more than happy to comply.

So, when John Senior got the nod to clean the windows of The Silver Palace, only the glitziest, most-glamourous joint in town, not to mention the tallest, John Junior was over the moon.

From poor stock, he had never set foot inside the door of a movie theatre before. So it was such an honour to get to be the one to polish and shine those magnificent tall windows. Like jewels they were, catching the first and last light of the day in all its splendour. This majestic towering light-house that mirrored and cast the sun's glow far across each soot-blackened terraced roof and the narrow winding cobbled streets leading off the square. The light projection gilding the slums around it. And so it was, that the night before, John didn't close an eye, being so jittery and excited. To him, this must have been what Christmas was like. Even the name of the place made him catch his breath in awe.

Being the youngest of a large family who, for the most part, lived off the clippings of tin, John envied all his friends who frequented the picture house of a weekend, for a matinée or early showing of the latest Hollywood extravaganza. They talked of nothing else from the moment it first opened its doors. Tales of cowboys and raven-haired starlets on the most-amazing adventures, with big names like Elizabeth Taylor and John Wayne on everyone's lips but his. Epic stories of war and romance, which crossed the big silver screen and had enthralled movie-goers the world over, but that he, John the window-cleaner's son, knew nothing about. It had long been his dream to save up enough money to go to see such a picture, but this was the next best thing.

The rest is history. Anyone around these parts will tell you. It was a match made in heaven, just like in the movies.

Her name was Constance - Connie to us - the oldest daughter of the town's finest victualler and highly thought of man about town. That same afternoon, John and his father were finishing up. She and her silly younger sister, dressed to the nines in new frocks, hats, and white gloves, had shown up an hour before the first screening, eyes out on sticks as if going to seek audience with the Queen. A vision in pretty lace and ribbons. And Constance, of course, looked as if she should be gracing the Silver Screen herself. She was such a beauty back then.

In complete contrast, poor John, tired, wet, and bedraggled after a full day of climbing and slopping buckets of water up and down the ladder to his father - spilling as much, if not more of it over himself in the process - was feeling quite deflated. The initial glamour had worn off the job. As luck would have it, on his last weary descent, he slipped and lost his footing, sending a wave of dirty slop all over the fine gowns of the aforementioned young ladies. Of course, angry at the horrific destruction of their elegant apparel and the ruination of their big event, John came in for a severe tongue-lashing, mostly from the younger miss.

But it was Constance, in floods of heart-broken tears, that affected him the most. It was, after all, she who had saved all of her money from doing the books for her father, to splurge on the expensive finery her mother would never have approved, not to mention the two precious movie tickets. She was therefore understandably quite inconsolable.

Needless to say, John melted when he saw the tears. Mannerly young lad that he was, in a costly act of contrition, he promised the distraught Constance a new dress, even offering to take her to the pictures himself on a more suitable occasion, to atone for his crime. He knew he'd get an earful from the *auld lad* for such wasteful extravagance, but to John it was more than worth his father's wrath, just to see her smile.

His first date, and hers, too, as it happened, was a life-altering success that quickly spawned into a weekly assignation that lasted right up until the day she died. She was twenty-seven. His one true love was tragically taken from him during childbirth, along with their first-born. It nearly killed him. At her funeral, it was so hard looking on, so cruel to see this beautiful strong man, broken and bowed at the front of mass, as if all his bones had melted, with all the air pressed out of him like a punctured balloon. When he looked up, people were appalled at his transformation, from handsome giant to a shrinking shell of a man - a walking ghost - all light and sparkle gone from his eyes, replaced with deep dark pools of loss. For the longest time, he spoke to no one.

But after a while, John found solace, returning to The Silver Palace week after week, as if watching a movie was a depiction of his own great love story projected onto the big screen in his head, a collection of all the wonderful moments spent there with Constance. Memories that somehow brought him back from the brink of despair.

And though the Palace has long since fallen silent, he still makes the journey. The building remains intact - tall and imposing - a testament to fine architecture despite long years of neglect. He still sees the beauty in it, remembering the glamourous history captured forever in its bones. A mausoleum to a golden era.

And so he pours all his love and longing into the roses he grows for her there, and I can only watch, just as I have always done. All these years, and he has never really noticed me. Plain Jane, the silly younger sister, who so harshly lashed out at him that first day. Oh, I've tried. I've stood here on the front step of our old family shop, our home, now mine, year after year, watching his almost pathetic weekly pilgrimage unfold. And we have talked - we have tea and cake after Sunday mass on occasion - but all he does is speak about her. His only reason for engaging my company is to share memories of their time together.

And the irony of it all is, it was I who shook the ladder from under him with my shoe that day. The silly, giddy younger sister, mooning over the hunky window washer she already knew and fancied, and had simply knocked the ladder to get his attention. That John, the big strapping lad with the broad manly chest and cheeky blue eyes that I have continued to dream of and watch from afar for so long.

Sadly, I still hold onto my earliest memories of him and what could have been - the leading man and star of all my internal movies, not this lonely old man he has become. My John, the kindest, most beautiful and most thoughtful young lad, who called to our shop for his mother's victuals every Saturday morning, when I, and not Constance, helped father to wrap the meat. She couldn't bear to get her hands dirty. But I was so glad I did.

Love is rarely like it is in the movies. Happy endings are a myth. In my head, I have always been his leading lady. After seventy odd years, perhaps it's time to give up waiting in the wings and bow out.

The Red Velvet Box

Mary T. Bradford

I watched her hands, tissue-like with age spots, blue veins peeping through. Now and then she paused by some trinket on a shelf or beneath a framed photo on a wall. Her pale grey eyes sparkled as she walked around her home, hummed songs from her youth.

"Some enchanted evening, you will see a stranger..." she sang softly.

"Are you sure you don't want to take some more bits and pieces from here with you, Ethel? There's plenty of room at the... I mean, at your new living place." I struggled to say retirement village.

"I've everything I need, Melody. My red velvet box is packed, isn't it?" She looked at me with flashes of mild horror. Fear that I may not give her the correct answer swam within them.

"Yes, I showed you where I put it. Remember? Wrapped in one of your scarves."

A contentment washed over the air between us.

"A cup of tea?" I asked.

"Something a bit stronger? It is a special night." She smiled.

I went and poured a large port for her.

Ethel sat in her favourite armchair, a faded green pattern, with some of the cushions ripping in parts.

I settled on the nearby sofa. While she sipped, I looked around the room and wondered how long it would take me to clear it out. Where would I find homes for all the contents? Charity shops would take only so much, and I wasn't really into the up-cycling way of life. Still, I could wonder about all that another day. Tonight, I needed to attend to Ethel.

"You look troubled, Melody?" Her cheeks were slightly flushed from her port, the drink warming her up.

"Me? Not at all."

"Listen, my dear, what's for you will not pass you. Love will always find a way. Look at me?" She placed her glass on the pretty side table, then pulled one of the jewel-coloured shawls she crocheted herself around her shoulders. "Now, listen to me. Love is a wonderful thing and, well, patience is important."

She was on a ramble. She sometimes did this – start one of her stories, and halfway through, her thoughts would forsake her.

Arranging for Ethel to go to the retirement home had been time-consuming. At times, she was so excited about moving, the day could not come fast enough. All she ever requested was to be taken to Butterfly Gardens when the day came, and that her red velvet box would go with her. It never left her sight – always nearby. I often wondered what was in the special box. A deep-purple ribbon was wrapped around it and tied in a funky bow-style.

"Ethel, can you tell me what's in the box?"

"The box, dear? What box?"

"Your red velvet box, the one with the purple ribbon?"

"Ah, Melody, it's great you should ask me that. For I was about to tell you." She sipped some more port and settled back in the chair. "Melody, love will find its way. No matter what. Love found me."

"Yes, you and William had a happy marriage." I pulled my feet beneath me on the sofa.

"Oh, I'm not talking about me and William, oh no. We were happy, we plodded along, and life was good to us. No, my dear, I loved William for sure, but I was not *in* love with him. There's a difference."

This was a bombshell. Had I heard right?

"It happened when I least expected it. I was in a book-exchange group that encouraged us to post a book to a member of another group once a month. I treasured it, like in a penfriend sort of way. Well, a member and I discovered we had a lot in common. Our dreams, our hopes, our wishes all connected. It was like we were one. We both felt that, up until then, our lives had been missing something and we had not known it until we met."

She sipped some more, her face alive with the joy of sharing this story.

"We wrote to and fro for a long time, never thinking we could meet up for real. Our letters were pages and pages long. Each moment of our day jotted down for the other to read. The everyday stuff, you know – if he cut the grass, if I met a friend for coffee. My friends became his and his became mine. I would tell him all they were up to. It made life alive sharing all these mundane yet important snippets for him of how my days passed. His rambling letters were filled with his doctor's appointments, his efforts at decorating his apartment, even financial matters. Like a child at Christmas, each letter brought joy. When a letter would arrive, I'd go to my favourite chair and wrap myself in a shawl, just like tonight, then, after I admired his handwriting on the envelope, I would trace my fingers over it."

Her spindly fingers roamed over an imaginary letter in her lap. I remained hushed.

"Then, after savouring his touch on the envelope, I would hold the sheaves of paper and inhale. I would start at the beginning, reading every word. How he addressed me was vital for me. It could be, *My Darling Ethel,* or *Ethel, my Love*, or simply, *Hello, M'Luv*. Oh, how it set my stomach in knots, his treasured words of endearment. I read it through and then I would let it sink in, his measured words, his thoughts and feelings, his whole being displayed openly on the pages for me to receive. And did I receive them! I lapped up each word, each syllable, and each stroke of the pen. I could no longer accept William's indifference to my interests. It showed me the gap that lurked between us. We were paddling along with each day."

Her face clouded over. Maybe giving voice to her secrets made her feel guilty.

"Are you okay, Ethel?"

"Oh yes, Mel, never better. Now where was I?"

"You and William were in a rut?" I offered to juggle her memory.

"But we stuck together. Till his death parted us. What we think is love, is nothing like the real thing. Melody, I admire that you have never settled for the first man to come along. Am I right?"

She sat upright in her chair and looked at me, her stare meaning business. This was serious to her.

I had never thought of such matters before. Yet, she was right – I was picky.

She smiled now, relaxed again in the armchair, sure in the knowledge she knew she was speaking the truth.

"Love, real love, is a splendid passion. When you wake in the morning and before you close your eyes at night, he is on your mind each time and every moment in between. I see you look at me like I've lost my marbles, but I can assure you I'm all there. Have you wondered at all, Mel, why I'm so happy to leave here?" Her expression softened. "I'm sorry, my dear, I'm not letting you say a word."

I didn't want to say a word. I wanted her to continue, sure there was more about to be spilled before this evening was over.

She sighed, then gazed around her. Searching. It had to be for the velvet box. It would be marvellous to see her love letters, the handwriting that she loved to touch and dream over.

"Do you want your box, Ethel?"

She nodded, tears glinting in her eyes. 'Look at me being silly. I should be happy – so happy.'

***

She slowly undid the ribbon, letting the purple organza slip through her fingers. A sereneness crossed her face and clothed it in a special something. Was this the true love she spoke about? I watched how she folded the ribbon and placed it aside on the table. Then she caressed the soft velvet, worn in parts from the countless times she must have gone through this ritual. Lifting the cover, she glowed with complete happiness.

One by one she took them out. They looked faded and worn-looking as she placed them on her lap, the box then put to join the folded ribbon.

"When he first sent me these, I laughed so loud. Look, how big they are!"

Her laughter was magical, and I too joined in. Knickers, six or seven pairs of knickers!

"He said in his letter how he wished he could be near me all day every day, and he believed this was a good but different way he could do it. Oh, he has such a sense of wickedness. A cocky grin and a heart so big, I couldn't help but love him. When I told him that, although I loved his choice, one or two of them were so big they almost came up to my armpits. So what did he do? He went and bought these, the romantic rascal."

She held up some smaller-style knickers: black with white trim, a sexy peach lace one, and a white pair with a star print.

"So I had a pair for each day of the week. And do you know what? I loved wearing them. When I slipped them on each morning, it was like he was giving me a hug. The satin material clung to my hips and up to my waist. It was like his hands were holding me close. I always felt loved when I wore them. Then, after a while, before they became threadbare,"—she giggled like a teenager in love—"I decided to put them away. So I did, in this box, wrapped in tissue. If ever I feel down or old, I take them out and remember."

She was growing tired now.

"Why don't we go to bed, Ethel. We've an early start in the morning."

"I suppose you think I'm quite mad. Saving pairs of knickers in a special box."

"No. I think it's beautiful. Having something so special that was shared, like you and...?"

"Babu, he's my Babu."

***

Ethel did not cry leaving her home. She stood at the gate and thanked the big house for all the happiness shared there. Her prized box sat on her lap as she settled inside the car. The drive was five hours, but she did not want to stop for tea or a toilet break.

"I've waited for this day for so long, I don't want to waste another minute."

The retirement home sat on a hillside, close to a beach. Its views over the bay were spectacular according to the brochure, and a waiting list existed for those who wished to live there. Ethel had her name down for years, she told us during one Christmas dinner. When the family asked why so far away, she just smiled and said nothing.

***

Pulling up outside the home, I could see why she'd picked the place. The grounds were beautiful, the retirement homes nestled beneath some giant firs – safe and cosy looking.

"Oh, Mel, this is so exciting. I finally get to be with him." She opened her door and hopped out like a lamb in springtime.

"With who?" I reckoned she was confused – tired after the journey. I went to retrieve her suitcases.

"There he is, there he is. Waiting."

I stopped what I was doing. When I looked up, I saw him, rushing towards the car, a cane in his left hand and a smile so large, it was obvious to all who witnessed their embrace that they were in love. So this was why she'd chosen Butterfly Gardens. Tears streamed down my face as I watched them hug, kiss, and touch each other's hair and face, not believing they were finally together.

Ethel turned and, with her arm linked in his, walked towards me.

"Melody, I want you to meet my Babu.'

Missing Pieces

Denis Ahern

You reach a certain age in your life and you begin to realise how short it is.

You begin to care less what people will say or what people will think.

You begin to question what you have done and what you have or haven't achieved.

You will think of the memories that you have made and the people that were there with you.

You will wonder what happened to most of them and why they aren't in your life right now.

You will begin to ask yourself are you happy.

If you are not, you will begin to question how come and what can you do to make yourself happy.

You will begin to question where did you lose yourself along the way.

What made you lose your spark?

Were you brave enough to follow your heart or were you too afraid of what others would think of you?

Were you simply afraid of getting hurt?

Were you tied to life's expectations?

As time moves on, you will begin to search for the memories that made you feel alive, the small ones that made you smile, the big ones that brought a tear to your eye, you will search for some memories that are so far out of your reach where you just cannot quite remember the words that were said but you remember exactly how those words made you feel in that moment, you will remember that smile and that look in their eyes that brought a warmth to your heart and a calmness to your mind.

You will close your eyes and wish for just one more moment, but you had so many happy times together that you cannot just pick one. Flashes of all your firsts together, from tight moments in the back of the car, the first time they reached out to hold your hand, the first weekend away to the nerves you felt going on the first date. You will be thankful for how you savoured each kiss, when your breath became one, you will remember how slowly you opened your eyes, looked into theirs and smiled.

It was as if time stood still, nothing else that was going on in your world mattered anymore and you captured this moment in your heart forever more. Even though the face is fading, you remember those eyes that made you feel alive, like you were all that mattered.

As you get older, love those who truly deserve all your love with your soul, because when the memories start to fade and when your heartbeat slows, your spirit will always remind you of who you were back then.

If you are lucky enough to find your missing piece, the person who feels like home, the part of you that was missing that you never realised you needed, the person where you cannot imagine a time when they were not in your life and you cannot picture a future without them, do not let your missing piece go. Some things only come once in a lifetime, and nothing is more tragic than losing what could of made you whole.

Memories will fade, but the feeling of love will always remain.

Erase & Rewind

Claire O'Connor

Before the alarm sounded, an intercom announcement updated them on yet another local risk. Most of Marcella's colleagues grabbed their bags and rushed to find a place on the shuttle. Despite the warnings, she opted to walk. Since the seasons left, she often reflected on the constant low daylight – like living life in sepia. These dark and foggy days were normal now, throughout the year. The streetlights strained to illuminate a path for the trundle of workers making their way home in the shuttle or in their pods. Few walked with Marcella.

There were alerts of some kind every single bloody day, and nothing had happened to her so far. If she wanted to walk home on her own occasionally, why shouldn't she? It took a bit longer to get home to her cabin, but the walk would eat into the evening at least.

As she arrived to her gate, she heard a beep behind her. Over her shoulder, she saw her neighbour Phil, with his annoyingly white teeth, hovering close by in his pod. She smiled and waved like the disingenuous cow she'd become, before hitting the enter button. Keeping her eyes to the front, she watched the door slide up. Little Ruby ran out, hyper and rolling around in excitement, tail wagging so hard her ass wagged too.

"Hello, girl." She ruffled her hair and gave her a good scratch behind the ears.

"Marcella, there's a pirate warning," Phil said, using the coms so he didn't have to leave his pod. "Didn't you get the alert?"

"Ah, I read something," she shouted back, keeping it nonchalant. "What kind was it anyway?"

He scowled at her. "There's a memory pirate lose in the district. Is your head shield working?"

"Should be. Best get inside then."

Once in, she plonked herself on the sofa. She pulled out her phone and saw twenty-one alerts. The system was set so the alert repeated until you acknowledged receipt. She opened the last message, sent just minutes before, and replied with the standard *'receipt confirmed'*.

A second later, she received a follow up: Please carry out a test on your head shield and please reply with *'need shield help'* should you have any questions or issues.

She sighed. The last thing she wanted was a technician at her door. All she felt like doing was baking her pizza ration and opening her wine pack. She'd been keeping the rations so she could have a good old drink some night. It helped to have a blowout once a month and today felt like the right day.

When the heating was on and she'd changed into her loungewear, she preheated the oven and unpacked her pizza – a synthetic grain base, with some kind of faux-tomato paste, reminiscent of the traditional Italian pizza. She liked it much more than the curries and stews they mimicked. Before 'The Panic', she'd attended a fascinating course about the history of food. Back then, the government still hoped to bring some original seeds back, but the virus wiped that idea out, along with so much more.

By late evening, she lay on the sofa, her eyes wet, the photo frame thrown on the floor, still on auto-flick. Ruby jumped up to lick her salty tears. Marcella often wondered whether the dog tried to console her, or she just liked the taste. It was still so hard to believe she'd gone from being a wife and mother to a lonely middle-aged woman with a needy dog, in just two years.

Wine pack empty, she sat up and heaved a huge sigh. She needed to prepare some things for work tomorrow, and check her head shield, wherever it was. After running upstairs to the storage closet, she hunkered on her knees and pulled out bags and boxes. A little cloth bag fell into her lap – his favourite blue silicon shoes, made like the old lace-up joggers that were popular in the 2000s.

With her head in her hands, she allowed the waiting sobs run free.

An alarm went off and she jerked up, looking around to find its source. Was it in the house? From the top of the stairs, she spotted her front door rising, despite it being locked securely behind her. She'd have to shut it off and open it manually in the morning. Spotting the shield on the top shelf, she grabbed it and ran down the stairs. Ruby skipped down in front of her and darted out the gap. Marcella pulled the shield over her head as she rolled under the door. Where the hell was the power button on this thing? She felt around the side of the helmet as she went. It wasn't on the other side either.

Looking up, she spotted Ruby running down the road, full of beans. The poor thing hadn't walked in three days. Standing just outside the door, she felt her way around the metal hood with her fingers, still searching for the button to activate the shield. Feck it, there's no one around. She sprinted as fast as she could down the quiet avenue.

When she caught up on the little dog, she swiped her up in her arms. As she straightened, ready to run again, she felt a shadow pass over her and looked up to see a dark figure towering above, blocking the dim streetlight. Before she had a chance to react, a flash of light pierced her eyes. The skin on her face tightened as her pores closed up with the heat.

Squinting against the glare, she sprinted back to her door, having just about enough space to roll in under it. Once in, she hit the button in a frenzy, but the helmet was dead. Letting herself fall onto the bottom of the stairs, she grabbed Ruby tight, rocking her. Losing Ruby was unthinkable.

***

The next morning, she checked her phone first thing as usual. The alerts! Apparently, there'd been a memory pirate in the area.

"Marcella are you okay?" someone called as she left the house.

She looked over at Phil, who stood watching her with concern.

"Absolutely, Phil. Anyone get hit by the memory pirate yesterday?"

He stared at her in disbelief for a moment, then walked towards her. "You did."

She laughed. He wasn't usually so funny. "Yeah. Right."

"Marcella, you need to go to the clinic. I saw you from my window last night. You were chasing Ruby, and he got you."

"What the hell are you talking about?" She shuddered as something came back to her about Ruby running off.

"He got you. You had your shield on, but it obviously wasn't working. Didn't you test it? Well, you won't know." His eyes pierced hers and she looked away, her head feeling like cotton. She'd worked. Came home and had wine. She remembered that.

"I-I remember. I do."

"What do you remember? You'll have some short-term memories for a while, they say."

"This is ridiculous." She shook her head in denial.

"Your long-term memory is gone, I think. Do you remember your childhood? Your family?"

It only took a moment before she gasped. Her head was blank. The nausea hit hard, and she leaned over to vomit.

"Shall I bring you to the clinic?"

"What can the clinic do?"

"You have to register what happened and get checked over at least. I'm sure there's a protocol. I've heard they can sometimes claw back certain periods, or people. It's worth a shot."

***

The doctor sat opposite her, speaking with a kind but firm tone. "We've sent the head shield off for testing. If we know the non-functioning area, we may be able to tell which part of the brain was more affected."

Marcella sat in silence, numb to it all. No memories meant nothing to reflect on – no points of reference at all.

A buxom nurse brought her to a small room where they put a kind of helmet on her.

"Okay, darling, not too much longer now." She patted her arm. "We're going to give you a potent mineral shot to see if helps."

"How?"

The nurse did the shot with ease, a set smile on show at all times. "Depending on the type of sabre used, it can continue to damage neurons. In some cases, these shots can stop that process in its tracks."

She wiped the injection spot. "Next, I'm going to ask you a series of questions. Some may seem repetitive, and some may be obvious. This is to gauge the damage."

The nurse's monotone voice and the annoying smile began to irritate Marcella. She didn't need to be patronised. She needed to understand the impact.

After the twenty-minute test, she was ready to walk out. "Look, can you just please advise me what I need to do to get my memory back? What happens next?"

The nurse let her head hang to the side and pursed her lips. "Your memory is not recoverable, darling."

"What? How will I go to work? How will I remember where I live, or who my friends are?"

The nurse looked into her eyes, waiting for a reaction, but Marcella hadn't quite digested the reality.

"Marcella, the damage has been done. It seems it was an old model sabre. The mineral injection should help retain anything you still have – residual – memories, short-term memories – but that's it."

She sat up in the chair, her chest heaving, her throat gripped by panic. "Do you understand what I am asking you? How do I get back to my normal life!"

The nurse sucked in a sharp breath. "You need to build a new life now."

Marcella growled and shook her head. What alternative universe am I in?

"You will be assigned a memory carer," the nurse continued, "who will train you in your daily tasks. They'll accompany you to work, introduce you to your friends and family, and feed your mind with things from your past so you can build a life again."

Marcella tensed as the panic flooded up through her body.

"D-do I have a family?"

The nurse picked up her file, and her eyes widened. "No, you have no family."

After several more tests and analysis, the nurse ordered her a snack. "I'll be leaving you now. The next memory carer available is Niall. He'll be along presently." She pursed her lips again and walked out of the room.

***

Marcella sat in the taxipod with Niall, her new 'memory carer'. He was chirpy, and annoying as hell. As he chattered about all the good things that were going to happen, her chest tightened as her anxiety rose.

"Eh, Niall, please! I think I need some quiet now. I need to go home and be alone for a while. I need to rest."

"Of course, but I will be by your side for at least the next thirty days. I'll even be staying in your spare room. My rations have already been redirected to your place." He grinned like a child as she rolled her eyes.

"I'll keep out of your way tonight. You must be very shocked. Tomorrow, we'll start working on your day-to-day routine."

***

Niall flittered around the kitchen, to her annoyance, getting his meal together. "I'm all done, so I can retire to my room. If you need me for anything, I'm here, no matter what it is."

He smiled at her, searching her eyes. "Do you remember how to use your dispenser? How to access your meals?"

Marcella followed his glance over to the chrome machine and stared at him, having no idea what he meant.

Twenty minutes later, they sat at the table together eating, as well as sharing their wine rations.

"You just need time to come to terms with it. I need time to assess what needs you will have, but you're not alone."

"How come I have no family? That doesn't feel right."

Niall flushed and looked down at his plate. "I'm not too sure, but plenty of women make that choice nowadays, given the current climate."

"No, but it doesn't feel like it's a choice I'd make. Something tells me I have people."

***

An hour later, Niall called the memory centre to check in.

"About the grief memory – I think we need to tell her the truth."

The silence down the line didn't last long. "It is protocol not to put anyone through the grief of losing loved ones again, even if they have lost their memory."

"But she knows. Somehow in there in her mind, she knows she should have family."

"Niall, you know the procedure. If she comes to you with specific questions, you can answer them. Otherwise, there was never a family. This is probably just some memory residue that will leave over the next few days.

***

Marcella, standing outside the door, heard it all. She ran to her bedroom, now alien to her, and scanned the room.

She looked up to see Niall at the door, his expression solemn.

"I'll tell you everything. Please come downstairs with me and let me give you something to calm your nerves while I explain."

"No," she moaned, holding up a photo.

"You can bring the photos. Please come on now. I'm here to help. I can tell you anything you need to know." He walked towards her and helped her to her feet, making sure the photos stayed with her."

***

Three hours later, she sat in silence staring out the window, with Ruby on her lap licking her swollen eyes. Her phone rang beside her, and she picked it up. Just about remembering how to use it, she opened a new message declaring her neighbourhood unsafe again, due to more pirate memories.

She sat at the window for the whole day while Niall faffed around in the periphery, making plans for the coming weeks: the training, the going to work, and the ordering rations. Every. Single. Bloody. Thing. He refused to get rid of the photos and clothes despite her asking several times. She did not want to remember anything else about it. She wanted to lose her mind, so she didn't have to feel like this anymore.

As the sun went down, she spotted the dark figure again, at the bottom of her street, striding up the avenue with determination. She ran out and shouted at him, with Niall calling her from behind.

Once she reached the tall, hooded figure, she stopped in front of him and looked up. "Do what you want! I don't want to remember anything anymore."

The familiar scorching flash blasted her again. She smiled and walked back to her house where Niall stood at the door looking down, his hand at his mouth.

Nothing Compares With You

Kerry Manning

Note from the author: After the sad passing of Sinead O'Connor, I was struck by these lyrics and how they could be turned into a story, in this case a love letter.

Dearest Olive

I have loved you for sixty years, and as I write this, I know that nothing, absolutely nothing could compare with you. Our love, although not always smooth sailing, was always true. We laughed so much, over silly things, and bonded over the incredibly hard and sad things, like losing your precious Rose. She lived for only 24 hours but has stayed with us for fifty years.

Today was her birthday, and silly man that I am, I ordered a cake, with pink rosebuds made from buttercream icing. Happy Birthday, Rose was piped into the middle just like we always did. I brought the cake with me when I visited.

For a minute, your eyes lit up and you clapped. "Party!" you said, before your eyes glazed over and your hands lay still on your blanket -covered lap.

Of course, I stayed, and the carers brought tea, and plates for the cake. I ate mine, and it landed like sweet sawdust on my tongue. You poked your finger in yours and licked it. The sweet stickiness brought a smile to your face, and that made me happy.

I wanted you back, even for half an hour, or a minute would do, to spend time wallowing in memories with me. I wanted you back to smile your cheeky smile when you found something funny. I pulled out the photo album from the bag for life, which I always seem to have with me. We started as we always do, turning the pages and telling the stories behind the photo squares containing our past.

It started as it always does, with the day I proposed and you showing off your ring. You were so proud of the sparkler and couldn't stop flashing it towards the light, creating rainbows for us to marvel at. It cost me a month's wages, but it was worth it, just to share your delight at our impending marriage.

I look at it now, still magical as it sits on your finger creating prisms. It was almost as though you could read my thoughts as you twisted it, held your hand up and smiled again.

We looked at the wedding photos, with you all in white like the princess you are. I loved you so much that day, but our love grew, didn't it?

We paged through, and you stared, but you weren't looking, were you, love? You were in a world of your own. Maybe a better world, where it hurt less.

As I turned the page to the one and only memory we have of you and Rose, on the morning she was born, you came back to me again, for a moment. You pointed your sticky finger at the plastic-wrapped page and said 'Rose', looking at me with a smile that lit up your eyes. And then you started crying. I think you remembered then, didn't you?

I turned the page, and you turned back inwards – perhaps safer there?

I left the rest of the cake for the carers and other residents, Olive; I think that is what you wanted. Then I packed the album back into the

Tesco bag and walked back to my car, my pace slow. It had been a good visit today.

Perhaps tonight I will treat myself to a small drop of whiskey, and another look at the photographs that chronicle our life together. We had the best of times, Olive. We really did.

Silent Wounds

Theresa Hiney Tingaal

"Keep quiet."
That is the mantra.
Who are these warlords? '
These keepers of secrets?
Do they wear the collar and the veil?
Evil being the anagram of veil, it says it all!
There's always a uniform,
something to hide behind,
something to strike fear.
Oh, Ireland,
how you made these mothers suffer,
along with their precious babies.
Beneath shame's heavy shadow
stitched into skin.
Woven through generations of pain,
their names mentioned in whispers,
their stories buried beneath guilt,
like pieces of filth.
Standing side by side, the church and the state,
against these mothers, was a campaign of hate.
Mothers and their babies endured a horrific fate.
With the fathers long gone, the mothers had to hide

behind walls of silence, where faith was meant to guide.
Oh, Ireland, my heart bleeds with sorrow,
for those who never knew a tomorrow.
Their dreams silenced before they could rise,
like echoes, swallowed by endless cries.
Beneath the weight of silent wounds,
lives shattered in forgotten rooms.
Their scars unseen, but always there,
etched into the land, into the air.
Whispers of the past still remain,
in an Ireland who traded its mothers for gain.
Burdened with a living bereavement, a lifetime of pain.

Remembering Ophelia

Carolann Copland

The rain was pouring down in strong, straight lines. Coming back home in the summer should have been a good bet but Killian was wading through pondlike puddles reflecting the lights from the side entrance of the pub. He pushed open the heavy door and stood dripping in the porch where the barman was arguing with a middle-aged woman.

"You can't smoke here."

"I'm not going out in that."

"Well, you're not smoking then."

Killian's phone pinged in his inside pocket and he unzipped his rain-soaked leather jacket to read the text. It was from his cousin to say he wasn't coming as the weather was so bad, and that he was sure Killian hadn't been mad enough to venture out himself.

"Well, fuck that," he said.

"Absolutely," the woman with the unlit cigarette joined in. "I've never seen anything like it. I drove down to collect the husband and his pals to save them from a drenching, and they say they're not ready to go home, so I've wasted my time. I can't have a drink because I'm driving, and now it looks like I can't have a smoke either."

Killian stared at her. "Sorry?"

"Nothing. Don't mind me. I'm only having a moan... Killian? No. Sorry, I thought you were..."

"Well, I am Killian. Killian Sullivan."

"I don't believe it. Do you remember me?"

Her face was familiar but the woman must have been a good bit older than him.

"You're looking great, Killian," she said. "You haven't changed a bit. Still got that baby face you had when we were at school."

"I'm sorry,' he muttered, 'I can't seem to..."

"Anna Donavan. I was your leading lady in Hamlet in our last year at school. Do you not remember the posters we had done up? Starring Killian Sullivan and Anna Donovan..."

"Anna Donovan?" He struggled to think of something nice to say. Not what was on the tip of his tongue, like: *"But how could you be Anna Donovan? You're old, middle-aged, and fat."*

"Anna, it's great to see you," he said. "How are you?"

"Stop gaping, Killian. Yes, I've aged. Like a fine wine. Married sixteen years, with four children and a chronic smoking habit. It's taken its toll. How about you?"

He tried to take all this in. Jesus, he couldn't have been gone that long. How could the stunning Anna Donovan, brilliant actress and singer, have ended up looking like... well, everyone else?

"Me?" he said. "I've no girlfriend right now and, eh, no children. Far too busy with work for all that. Spent a few years in the Westend in London, but mostly I've been singing my way through the theatres of Broadway. I'm back home for a few days, for my grandmother's birthday." He thought that sounded lame, so added, "And to catch up with a few old pals."

"You always said you'd be famous, Killian. Good on you. Hey, I'm going back inside. It's getting nippy, especially without a ciggy to warm me up. Are you meeting someone?"

"Yeah, well, no. My cousin, but he's ditched me. I suppose I'll head home."

"Come on in and have a drink with James and his friends. They're boring the pants off me. Secondary school teachers do nothing but give out about the teenagers in their classes. We can remind them how terrible we were at school."

He stood there, unsure, looking at her, still shocked at the transformation.

"But maybe you have better things to be doing," she said. "A man of your fame."

"No, not at all," he found himself saying, though he meant to say, *"Yes, he had lots to do."* Curiosity got the better of him, wanting to know who Anna had married and how she'd ended up like this. "You're right. I couldn't come all the way into town and then turn around and go home again. I'd love a pint."

Anna turned and he followed her into the half-empty pub, towards a group of men who were putting on coats as they stood around a table heaving with finished pints.

"James, do you remember this guy, Killian Sullivan, from my class?"

Killian recognised him right away. Mr Molloy, their geography teacher. He felt a telling off for non-compliance of homework was in the making.

"Ah, the great thespian himself. How are you, Killian? Sorry, Anna, we were about to leave. We're moving on to Jack's house for a night cap and a game of cards. It's a shame you dragged yourself out in this weather for nothing but... What possessed you? Anyway, we won't be long." He gave Anna a peck on the cheek, then the four lads nodded and waved and headed for the door.

"I'm going to stay and have a drink with Killian. See you at home," she called after him.

Killian looked at her, amazed that she didn't seem upset.

"He can't be your husband? Mister Molloy?"

"Has been for sixteen years."

"That's a long detention, alright. How did it all happen? I mean, when I left you at our Debs, you were full of plans for what you were going to do with your life."

He shed his sopping jacket on a nearby stool, delighted he'd worn his white Prada shirt to show off his tan.

"I'll get the drinks... I don't suppose you're still a Malibu-and-pineapple girl?"

"Go on. I'll have one for old time's sake." She smiled up at him and, for a moment, he saw something he remembered of his Ophelia there.

He shivered as he waited at the bar, and ran his fingers through his wet curls. Mr Molloy had been a bully at school. He'd been young, alright, for a teacher, but the power had gone to his head early. He lived for putting the great thespian in detention. Somehow, he had snared the lovely Anna Donovan and turned her into this woman, devoid of makeup, with messy hair, and the extra-large anorak thrown over the back of her chair. He took the pint and the Malibu and moved back to their table.

"So, did you come to any decisions about me while you were sussing me out in the mirrors behind the bar?"

She flashed him her roguish smile once more, and he had the good grace to look embarrassed. Her plain black T-shirt showed off some lovely curves. She'd let her pony tail out and her auburn hair nestled around her face.

"I'm jesting," she said, taking a sip of her malibu and grimacing. "The answer to your probable first question is, a baby. One of the girls in our class, I think it was Fiona, goaded me that I couldn't use my ample flirting skills to pull Mister Molloy. It became a game but one that ended up with me being pregnant. I think he wanted to hang on to his job at the time, so, he married me. The last sixteen years have resulted in three more babies and a relationship that isn't all that bad. We're great pals, me and James. We grew to love each other, and it's nice and easy. As for this evening's dress? Well, yeah, I find it hard to be bothered when I'm running around after teenagers and toddlers."

Killian tried to take all this in.

"Well... yeah, Anna. I'm a bit blown away, alright, but cheers. Here's to you and Mister Molloy, and all the little Molloys. So, did he mellow over the years?"

"Well, he's only seven years older than us, so, he possibly felt that he needed to be stricter than the other teachers to get our respect at school. He's nothing like that at home because he spoils the little horrors. I love them dearly but they could all do with an occasional bit of detention from their father."

"Right." He took a sip of his pint and scrunched up his face. In New York, he told everyone that you had to drink Guinness in the homeland, but... "I'm gobsmacked, to be honest, with you being married to Murder Molloy. I missed a big audition once for the Gaiety Theatre because of a detention he gave me. I could have made it big here in Ireland instead of having to travel to London so soon after school."

"Let me get this right, Killian. You're holding a grudge against my husband seventeen years after he gave you detention, and claiming that he stifled your career in acting? Killian Donovan, who never handed his homework in on time and got out of going to class at every given opportunity? You're hilarious. Though, to be honest, if this is going to be a slagging session of my husband, maybe we should drink up and go home."

"Sorry, Anna. I didn't mean to... Sure, what do I know?" He hadn't managed a decent relationship with anyone since... well, since Anna dumped him after the Debs.

"No-one special?" she asked. "Surely you've been wowing the chorus girls of Broadway for years?"

"If it's long and meaningful you're after, the chorus girls of Broadway are the ones to keep well away from, and sure, my career doesn't lend itself to long-term relationships." He sipped his stout again. Still not good. "So tell me, Mrs Molloy, is what you've got the best that life could've offered you?"

"Wow. There's a question, and I think the answer needs a little more lubrication. Same again?" She stood up, and her T-shirt rose up to show a fairly flat tummy, considering.

"Eh, no thanks. I don't think I'm a Guinness kind of guy after all. It tastes bitter. I'll have a..." He looked along the line of branded taps on the counter and tried to figure out what he wanted.

"Will I get a bottle of red?"

"No more Malibu and pineapple?"

"That was disgusting."

"What about your car?"

"I'll get a taxi, and James can get up and collect the car in the morning. Good enough for him."

Killian watched her at the bar, enjoying the view of her toned tush. He looked down at himself and pulled his shirt out over his jeans to hide his tyre. As she waited for the wine, Anna seemed to be sharing a bit of flirty banter with the barman. Getting back to their table, she swung one leg over the other stools and pulled her other one after it, without dropping the wine.

"Very impressive," he said. "Do I remember you doing the splits as a party piece years ago?"

"Still can, but maybe not here." There was that brilliant smile again, with the green eyes, full of mischief.

She poured wine into two glasses with well-practiced style, then handed him a glass and clinked it with hers. "Sláinte." She took a sip and sat back. "Now, that's more like it. I can't believe I used to drink that other shite. Older and wiser."

Killian took her cue and sipped his wine, thinking she may be older but she wasn't wiser. "So, Anna. What do you do when you're not being Mrs Molloy or Mammy Molloy? Is there life outside all that?"

"Oh, I always have some class or other going on. It's important to have time to myself at the end of the day."

"What kind of classes?" He smirked. "Adult education?"

"Well, I've tackled all sorts of things over the years but I seem to have settled into the pole dancing very well. It's great exercise, and James thinks it's dead sexy."

Killian reached for a coaster to mop up the drink he'd spilled down his shirt, making the red wine seep in more.

Over the next few glasses, Anna talked him through the various courses she had undertaken.

"My dad died ten years ago, in the hospice. They were wonderful to him, to all of us. So, every new challenge I take up now, I use it to do some fundraising for them. So far, I've parachuted out of an airplane, walked a tightrope across a waterfall, and swam with sharks. Don't look so surprised, I was in a kind of cage-like thing."

Killian sat wide-eyed, not able to think of one witty remark.

"Will you still be here on Wednesday?" she asked. "I've organised a pole-dancing extravaganza in our local pub. It's nearly sold out but I could get you in."

"Now, I know you're having me on." He was shaking his head and laughing but then she handed him a flyer from her coat pocket, with a picture of her dancing around a pole, wearing an incredibly sexy outfit.

"And Molloy's okay with all this?"

"Of course. It's for charity." She drank the last drop of her wine.

"Hah, I'll be there." He was thinking of settling in with another bottle when Anna got up and started putting on her anorak. He knocked back his wine and stood up.

"Better get on. Early mornings are a killer. It was great to bump into you, Killian."

"And you, Anna. Will I walk you to your taxi?"

"That'd be great. Thanks."

She zipped up and turned herself back into the woman who'd wanted a cigarette in the porch earlier but he knew now what was underneath, so to speak. He thought it might not be too bad to see a little more of the Anna under the anorak. That would be one in the teeth for Molloy. They walked out into the deluge and Anna attempted to light a cigarette. He put his hands on her shoulders to protect against the rain and wind, and she took a deep pull and exhaled contentedly. When he dropped his hands to her waist and leaned down to kiss her, she stepped back, a look of amused disbelief across her face.

"Tell you what, Killian, it'd be as easy for me to walk to the taxi rank on my own. Thanks all the same. And, eh, don't worry if you can't make Wednesday. Good luck with the acting and everything."

He watched his Ophelia stride towards the main road, pulling her anorak hood up around her head. As he stood there, he wished he hadn't met her now. Better to have kept the beautiful memory of who she used to be.

"Fuck that," he said as he zipped up his useless leather jacket and dragged himself towards the last bus home, to suffer more slings and arrows of outrageous fortune in his sadly lacking love life. "Her loss."

Doubt

Sandra Matthews

Rich in faces
    Poor in names
    Memory makes sometimes dubious claims

He recalls
So do I
Together we were under same azure sky
No, no it was dull grey
Or so he very dares to say
He's wrong
He's wrong
I must be right
With my own eyes I saw that sight

I say blue
He says grey
His honesty I do not doubt
His memory is simply out
Out of sync
Out of whack
Might I suggest this using tact?

REWIND COPY

Or could it be that I am wrong
Can I no longer trust the song
In videos played back to me
When mind and I ever agree?

Rich in story
Poor in fact
Memories trick and doubt attract

Fallow Ground

Martin Daly

Pat Buckley stood beside his wife, Rose, at the foot of their garden. He bore a studious expression. It was a Saturday. Earlier, over breakfast, he had nodded towards the overgrown plot outside the kitchen window.

"I'll tackle it today," he said. "It's time to turn that soil."

"Don't make me laugh, Pat – I've been hearing that one for years. You've never sunk a spade as much as once since I moved here."

"You're right, Rose – but it's lain fallow long enough."

"I'll believe it when I see it. I've got a mind to get a gardener in."

"I'll never allow that!"

"It's your choice."

Pat went to the tool shed, ignoring a young boy sitting on the garden wall, kicking his heels. He seemed familiar, in his short pants and a hand-knit sweater over a shirt with a shabby collar. When Pat re-emerged, he'd disappeared.

The park of council houses was built in blocks of five or six near Douglas village in Cork during the Fifties. They were sturdy houses with bathrooms, hot and cold running water, and a front and rear garden. Pat and Rose lived there, as did Pat's mother, Alice – a widow.

His grandparents Mick and Mary were the original tenants. Mick, an only child, was raised in a decrepit village cottage and was orphaned at age sixteen after his father dropped dead and his mother passed away from grief not long after. He continued to live in the cottage and found work as a weaver in the local mill, where he met Mary, a darner. They married, and Joe, their son, was born at home. Because of their living conditions, the Council gave them a new house – an end-of-terrace house with extra garden space at the gable end. Mick loathed the noise and the dusty, fibrous mill air, and his happiest hours were spent working outside.

Every autumn, he took a wheelbarrow and gathered the fallen leaves of sycamore trees not far from home. He mulched these beneath canvas sacking over the winter, then turned the soil in springtime and dug in the composted leaves. The back and side gardens were dedicated to vegetables. Mary worked the front garden, where she grew roses. It was all very orderly and much admired.

From their first days in the new house, Joe liked to work in the garden alongside his father. Mick enjoyed his company, and they developed a close bond. Until age sixteen, Joe had entertained notions of entering the priesthood. But after an enjoyable encounter with a girl on the hill above the village, all notions of celibacy were banished. He decided to become a bricklayer.

Marian, Mick and Mary's daughter, was born in the rear bedroom of the new house after a difficult delivery, and she suffered intellectual difficulties as a result of birth trauma. Her path into adulthood was difficult. The principal of the girls' school advised Mick and Mary that 'Poor Marian has little hope outside of the mill, God help her'. They considered this advice well-intentioned and sound, so on the first Monday after turning fourteen, Marian began work at the mill alongside other village girls who made her feel welcome.

She had always been shy and preferred a quiet life until she turned eighteen. Then – almost overnight – her personality changed. She began to wear make-up and style her hair, her long, tousled locks often obscuring her face. Mary disapproved, but Marian was insistent.

"I could wear my hair any way I wanted to in England!" she yelled, and the matter was settled. Mary backed off, and Mick merely rolled his eyes.

Marian began to frequent pubs, where Bacardi rum banished her shyness. She attended dances where she enjoyed herself until it was time to either accept a lift home or catch the bus. At this time, she also began a stream of short-term relationships, and developed a reputation as a girl of 'easy virtue'. Gossip reached the parish priest, who visited the home with words of caution for Mick and Mary. They felt that this visit reflected on them as parents. Later that evening, Joe was reading in his bedroom when he heard his sister screaming. He ran downstairs, but Mary prevented him from entering the front room.

"Your father is having a few words with Marian, Joe. You stay out of it." Later, while lying in bed, he heard his sister sobbing. On Monday, Marian went to work without comment.

Such strict rules didn't apply to Joe, of course. The 'golden boy' was young and handsome, his pockets filled with cash. He was popular with the girls and enjoyed every opportunity presented. Lack of judgment, or to be more precise, carelessness, and a disregard for the law of averages, led to Alice Sheehan becoming pregnant. Her father had a fiery reputation, and a hasty marriage was arranged over a visit to Mick and Mary. Joe and Alice moved to a small flat in Cork City and Alice gave birth to a boy they named Pat.

But Marian grew bored with life at home, and surreptitiously returned to her 'wild ways'. She soon announced her intention to leave for England.

"Over my dead body," replied Mick

"You can't stop me, Dad – I'm over eighteen!"

This declaration of independence drew an unmerciful hiding from Mick. Mary trembled outside Marian's bedroom door, crying tears of loss.

The next day was a summer Sunday. Mick and Mary attended mass, leaving their daughter alone, nursing both her wounds and her pride. Afterward, they took the bus to the seaside at Crosshaven. An ominous smell of gas greeted them at the front door that evening. Once inside, they had to push open the kitchen door. Marian's body lay on the floor, her head deep inside the gas cooker's oven.

Mary and Mick were both shattered, though Mick's stoic nature prevented him from displaying grief. He did, however, ask Joe to bring Alice and Pat to live at home, opining that the presence of another woman and a young baby might comfort Mary. Over time, a semblance of normality returned. Mick continued to work in the mill and his garden, but he now insisted that he work the garden alone. Joe was surprised and saddened at this turn of events.

"I *need* this, Joe. Turning the ground when I'm alone makes me feel less sadness – less guilt." Joe accepted his father's explanation. He was busy, anyway, helping Alice rear Pat, a lively boy, filled with curiosity.

Over the next two years, Mary grew thin and pale. She'd been a sturdy woman who rarely complained. The local doctor referred her to a specialist, who diagnosed her with terminal cancer. The end came within a year, and on a miserable, rainy morning, she was laid to rest beside Marian.

Four more years went by. One Saturday morning, Joe was raking leaves outside, Pat playing beside him. Mick emerged from the kitchen, his face red with rage.

"What the hell do you think you're doing, Joe? This is *my* garden – *my* work, dammit!" Pat saw his grandfather pick up a shovel. "Now clear off or I'll take the bloody head off you."

"Easy, Dad – I was only trying to help."

"I don't *need* your help!" roared Mick, his face purple as he swung the shovel. The handle caught Joe on the arm. Pat, frozen with terror, watched his father, shame-faced, with eyes downcast, walk away.

"Come on, Pat," muttered Joe with a forced smile, "We'll have some soft-boiled eggs with toast."

"Can we make soldiers of the toast, Dad?" asked a tearful Pat, referring to how Joe cut the buttered toast into narrow strips for dipping into the runny egg.

"We will, son. Soft-boiled eggs and a whole plate of soldiers."

Later that evening, Mick was piling up leaf mulch in the crisp glow of a streetlight when he felt a tightness in his chest. He struggled to breathe, and staggering towards the house, managed only a few steps before he fell facedown into a pile of leaves. The doctor told Joe he had died instantly – much the same as his father before him. From that day onwards, Joe never touched the garden, except to clear away weeds.

Joe, Alice, and Pat settled into an uneventful, comfortable life. Pat grew up and went to university, and his parents were proud when he was honoured with a Doctorate in Biology. He began to travel the world on a fellowship, researching butterflies.

On one visit home, his mother challenged him on his bachelor status.

"Y'know, Pat, you're almost thirty-three. Will I ever get to see a grandchild?"

"Ah, stop, Mam, will you?" He laughed. "The right woman hasn't shown up yet."

Alice sighed. "I wonder if she ever will."

Pat had inherited his father's proclivities for sexual gratification and made the most of all opportunities. Destiny, however, would have its way. On a Sunday visit to Fitzgerald's Park, he was startled when a woman sat across from him at the table where he was reading a periodical.

"I'm sorry," she said, "but there are no empty tables. May I share this one with you?"

"Please," he replied, taking in her smiling face, and bright-blue eyes. "Isn't it a nice day for the park, Miss?"

"I'm Rose," she said. "And it is."

"I'm Pat." That night, Rose and Pat lay together, conducting in-depth explorations of the mating habits of butterflies.

Rose worked in the city library. The courtship was intense and brief, and Pat soon invited her to meet his parents. Alice grew hopeful, while Joe admired Rose's easy elegance. They married the following year, whereupon Rose moved into the family residence.

After the marriage, however, Pat – inexplicably – lost all interest in sex. The couple remained childless. Whenever Rose reached out to him in tenderness, he muttered some excuse. He refused to discuss the matter and Rose grew increasingly frustrated.

Early one morning, screams of "Joe! Joe!" woke Pat and Rose from their sleep. Pat rushed to the adjacent bedroom. Alice was holding her husband's head in her lap. Like his father and grandfather before him, Joe had succumbed to a sudden heart attack.

Pat laid the tools on the concrete path, rolled up his sleeves, spit in his hand for increased grip, and picked up a slash hook.

"Will you manage it this year?"

He turned at the sound of the youthful voice and saw the boy sitting astride the wall, a grin dimpling his cheeks.

"Is it me you're talking to?"

"Who else is here, besides us?"

"Cheeky little git, aren't you?"

"I'm just askin' if you'll work the garden this year."

"Why wouldn't I?"

"You never managed it before, did you? I've watched this old routine year in, year out. You never get beyond cutting the weeds."

"Watch your mouth, lad. I have work to do." With that, he began to slash at the weeds and lay them in sullen clumps. He fell into a rhythm, and when he reached for the garden fork he noticed that the boy had disappeared. Within an hour, he'd cut and removed half of the weeds, piling them against the rear wall. Rose brought some tea.

"Fair play, Pat – that's a decent effort – if you can keep it up. Anyway, I'm off to town with Alice – we'll be home in time to make dinner."

"See you later," said Pat.

"That's it for the day, so?"

Pat turned his head.

"You're back?"

"I never left."

"Don't tell lies – I saw that you'd gone."

"No, I didn't. Anyway – finish your tea and get back to work, ok?"

"You're one cheeky brat. Do you live around here?"

"I do."

Ignoring the boy, Pat attacked the remaining half of the garden. These weeds fell easier, and the entire side was soon cleared. His hands hurt, and he decided to go and look for gloves. He couldn't find any.

"Are you finished, so?" came the irritating voice from the wall.

"Jesus, you're still at it. How old are you?"

"I'm seven, and all I asked you was if that's it again until next year."

"What do you mean by 'again'?"

"It's what I see every single year. You clear the weeds, and that's it then until the following spring. Maybe your wife will get someone in to do it for you."

"So you think I can't do it?"

"I think you're afraid to."

"And why would I be afraid?"

"Ghosts, maybe. You're afraid you might dig up a few ghosts."

"Hold on a second," said Pat, after a short pause. "You said that you're seven years old?" "That's right."

"And how long have you been watching me in my garden?"

"For over thirty years now."

In a flash of memory, Pat recalled the episode when he'd witnessed his father being assaulted and shamed, and then ordered out of the garden. And he remembered that he was seven at the time.

"My name is Pat," said the boy. "Do you recognize me now?"

"Yes – yes, I do," he replied, tears streaming down his face. "And there *are* sad memories buried in this ground. Ghosts, as you say."

"All that grief and guilt belonged to your grandfather," said the boy. "It didn't belong to your father, nor does it belong to you. Lean on the strengths of your ancestors, not on their weaknesses."

"Who sent you?" asked Pat.

"Nobody – I've always been beside you. Traveled the world with you. Your shadow. I took care of you. Protected you – mostly from yourself, by the way. Oh, the antics you got up to!"

Pat sank the fork into the ground and turned the first sod. He worked steadily, and within a few hours, he'd turned the entire garden. He ignored the blood between his fingers and the red streaks along the wooden handle. He glanced towards the wall when he was done.

"Thanks for taking care of me."

"You're welcome."

"I'm hungry," said Pat. "Fancy a soft-boiled egg?"

"With soldiers of toast?"

"A whole plate full of soldiers. We'll share them."

Rose was surprised when she and Alice returned home and saw the garden. She found Pat asleep in an armchair, his hands wrapped in a towel, and a scattering of vintage children's comics on the floor.

"Pat!" she cried. "Your hands!" She bathed his hands in warm water, dried them gently, and wrapped them in gauze. "How did you manage to finish it all?" she asked.

"A little boy helped me," he replied, unable to hold back a gentle smile.

"That was nice of him. Was it one of the neighbors? I was wondering why the old comics

were out."

"You'll meet him soon."

Together that night, they cultivated fallow ground. They nurtured it, and shortly after Christmas, Rose delivered a baby boy.

"What name will you give him," asked Alice, holding her longed-for grandchild.

"Mick", Rose answered.

"A mighty name," added Pat.

And never again was there any talk of an outside gardener.

End of The Road

Aislín O'Neill

You went out to buy some fizzy water. You were sure that was it, until you weren't sure. No longer sure about a lot of things, definitely not sure about where you'd been for four hours on that Monday in January. You'd made the decision to stop driving in the dark. The straining to see in the blackness and the bright lights of the cars made your eyes water. You were sensible, knew your limitations, and stuck to daytime outings. You loved driving and your independence.

You were armed with a list of two things: buy fizzy water for your wife and speak to the pharmacist about your blood pressure tablets. You had a plan. What could go wrong?

I'd popped up to visit on the Saturday before the trip. You'd told me what you'd read about your medication in the newspaper. I rarely listened now. The visit was more duty-driven than pleasure. I didn't take tea. I didn't take water, even the fizzy kind. You offered both, plus the story about your childhood dog Sinbad, who'd run away to sea. I didn't listen for the punchline. I'd heard it before. Looking at my phone more than at you, I missed so much. I nodded in the right places, or so I thought. Maybe you were thinking differently in those moments when you were quiet. I said I needed to pick up my daughter – your grandchild – from a friend's. I didn't need to. I needed to escape.

You'd looked disappointed. You mumbled something about my busy life and how hard it must be for me, juggling everything.

You told me how grateful you were, how good I was, and how you loved seeing me. I felt guilt, a surge of unadulterated guilt. I held it deep inside and carried on out the door, into the welcoming air of the crisp morning, chasing the smell of decay from my nostrils.

You left at 3.30 p.m. For three hours, I didn't know you were missing. The call came from your wife of fifty-nine years. She'd been ringing you. Over and over, she'd said.

You'd answered once. Whilst driving, I found out later – another reason to berate you. In that call, you said you'd seen a road sign to Saintfield.

You said you had to go then, so you could concentrate on the road.

You also said it was very dark and the car lights were so bright. Another hour would pass before a call came from a garage attendant, in Downpatrick, telling me you were with him. Google maps talked me through the forty-five-minute journey to find you. I was grateful for the company.

I saw you before you saw me – your expression one of unsurety. I had arrived at the garage looking for my father. I found someone who looked very much like him.

You were pleased to see me. You'd been chatting to the attendant. You loved to chat, to tell your stories from the past, from a time when I didn't know you and you didn't know me. I forget exactly when I'd stopped listening.

You didn't want to leave your car behind, insisting you'd be fine to drive it back. You became over animated in your retelling of what was quickly becoming your 'big adventure'.

You couldn't foresee the future repercussions. You needed a lot of persuasion to come with me.

You'd gone out in the dark all by yourself. At first, I was quick to accuse you of breaking your own rule. I talked at you, telling you off as I might a child, for this failure to behave.

You asked me not to be cross – a childlike plea which caught me unawares.

You had fallen short of my expectations and I made it clear. You insisted you'd stuck to your rule; it was daylight when you left our old family home, a five-minute drive from your destination.

You said I was shouting at you. Maybe I was.

You hadn't taught me how to deal with something like this – this role reversal. Now, I had to tell you what to do and that just felt wrong.

It was half past eight when I finally dropped you home. Your wife asked where her fizzy water was. She was cross with you for leaving it in your car; your happiness at being home dissipated. You hated to let anyone down. I bit my tongue, wanting to get away. I'd be back in the morning for a trip to the doctors. As I headed away to my car, I looked back and caught a glimpse of people I used to know.

When the doctor asked, you couldn't remember why you'd gone to the shopping centre. Your face showed the concentrated effort you were making to recall some iota of information to make sense of it all. You looked at me, silently beseeching me to fill in the gaps. I desperately wanted you to appear normal. On that we were agreed, I think.

You told the doctor you loved the freedom of the road, that you were a great driver – no accidents ever. You wanted to prove it had all been a mix up, that you were fine, just your usual self. When had you last been your usual self? I had long ago absented myself, physically and emotionally. I'd missed the change – the transition.

You remembered why you'd gone to the pharmacist. You'd decided to stop taking your tablets, the ones that kept your blood pressure stable. You'd read something in the paper that said they had side effects. So, you'd stopped on Saturday, just like that.

You'd wanted to show the pharmacist the article you'd cut from the paper, that was carefully folded in your wallet for safe keeping. The same article you'd told me about. If I'd paid attention, could I have changed the outcome, stopped the 'great adventure'?

You were referred to the TIA clinic at the hospital. You were told not to drive. I suggested I could take the keys in case you forgot. The doctor readily agreed. How had we arrived at this point so quickly?

If we thought things were getting worse, then Accident and Emergency would be our next port of call. I drove you home. We talked about the car, the keys, the adventure. You had already forgotten you wouldn't be able to drive. I took you through what would happen next. You told me how your father worked on the light ships and had never owned a car. You told me you'd never done a driving test.

You said you were a good driver. I agreed.

You insisted it was alright to leave the keys with you. You wouldn't use them. You promised. Your child-like pleading unnerved me. I tricked you into giving them over. I'd look after them, I told you. I felt the wrongness. What right did I have to deny this adult man his autonomy? I was the child. Your wife said there was no need to take the keys. Her life was now ruined because you couldn't drive. She would look after them. She wouldn't let you use them. I wasn't taken in by her promise. I took your keys. I took your licence. I walked away.

You couldn't wait for the appointment. Your wife couldn't wait. We went to A&E.

You were chatty on the journey. You told me about the white mouse you'd had as a boy that had mysteriously disappeared. I'd heard the story before. I knew the ending. It was the cat. I acted surprised.

You believed you'd be driving again after that visit. No amount of explaining would change that belief. You watched me scrolling on my phone, and said you were jealous of how much fun I seemed to get from it. You asked me to show you how to use yours. I showed you how to delete the three thousand unimportant emails you had – a repetitive but simple job that involved pressing two buttons. You managed to get rid of four before asking for help. Frustration fizzed inside me and surfaced as impatience in my voice.

You stopped asking after that, and just sat staring at your screen, like me and most of the others in the waiting room.

You said something, but I was engrossed in an unimportant tweet and missed what you'd said. You said it again. I looked up.

You said I was your favourite. I always had been.

You told me how pleased you were that I'd come home. I'd been away longer than I'd been at home. Belfast is always home, even when it isn't.

You couldn't tell me why I was your favourite, just that I was. At times, I'd craved to be the favourite – times before today. Now, I didn't want the burden. It implied responsibilities. I wanted to say I wished I'd stayed away. I'd come home to be with my father, but I couldn't find him. Instead, I'd found you, the pretender. I wanted to say this made me sad. I didn't. Instead, I told you that you were my favourite father.

You laughed. I didn't.

You got a quick referral for a brain scan the following morning. You joked with the young doctor, saying you hoped there was a brain to find. I loved your humour.

On the way back to the car, you asked if you could drive. I explained about the next hurdle.

"So, when they've done a brain scan, I can drive?" you asked.

"Maybe," I said.

You said you liked my car. You said you had one just like it.

When I dropped you off, you told your wife that you'd be driving tomorrow.

"Maybe," I said. "Depends on the scan."

You needed to placate her. I recognised in you a skill I'd honed to perfection: keeping others happy. You'd been doing it for thirty-one years more than me. You had led by example.

You'd taught me well. There was still so much more to learn. I wasn't ready to graduate.

You were waiting by the gate of your house the next morning when I came to take you for your brain scan. Wrapped up warm, wearing your favourite hat. The scan showed no sign of a TIA.

"Great," you said. "I can drive?"

You wanted to phone home to share the good news. I said the consultant would decide. She asked you questions – questions you thought silly. You laughed, trying to remember why you were there. What was the date? The year? The place?

You said she was trying to trick you. You laughed off what you didn't know, and said she wasn't going to get the better of you.

You couldn't remember your big adventure.

You had experienced an episode of amnesia. They weren't sure why. It might happen again. You were referred to your GP for a memory test, with no driving until diagnosis. We left. I said nothing. The bubbles of happiness dispersed. The next challenge was lined up.

"I'll be driving once I've done the memory test," you said.

"Maybe," I said.

You got a good price for your car. You hadn't taken much persuasion to sell. You already had your sights set on a smaller model, once you passed the memory test. The test had assumed giant proportions – the pressure to pass grew daily. I loathed the test. I loathed what you'd become. I did not loath you.

You struggled to transition into the world of taxis. The world of dependence. Explaining the costs of running your car didn't stop the complaining.

When I picked you up for your test appointment, your wife told me you weren't stupid. I told her it was not about you being stupid or not – it was about your memory. She didn't listen.

You didn't want me coming into the doctor's with you. You said you wouldn't be able to say what you wanted to if I was there. You wanted to tell the doctor that your life was ruined.

When we arrived, you wanted me to come in with you.

You did not tell the young doctor that your life was ruined. The doctor was pleased with you. I could see you sparkle. Your body unfurled. Tension dissolved. You'd been sitting on your hands, something I do when stressed. I saw the impact on you, my carefree father. I wanted to cry for you but didn't. Instead, I asked the question – the one that needed to be asked but could as easily not have been – the question that chased away a sparkling ending.

"Can he drive?"

You were smiling. I wasn't. What had I done? I'd had to ask. Still fizzing with success, I don't think you even heard. I was grateful. The doctor left to ask a colleague.

You wanted to buy a car straight away. I told you the doctor needed to call the Driving Agency. "Not today," she'd said. "Maybe next week."

"So, I'll be driving in a week," you said.

"You need to call on Friday," I explained. "She'll know more then."

"I'll not buy a car tonight then," you said on the way out.

On the journey home, you said you might just have to get your bike out. You didn't have a bike. You told me how you'd once cycled for Ireland, and how your best friend had flown over his handlebars and died instantly. You told me you used to have a car just like mine, except it was red.

You soon forgot. I did not forget the day I ended your independence.

"I'll be driving next week," you told your wife when I dropped you home.

"See, I told you he wasn't stupid," she said.

What could I possibly say? I walked away.

You said you'd forgotten you'd rung me. I was glad. Five missed calls in the space of an hour. No caller ID. I'd known it was you. I hadn't wanted to give you a lift to the shops. I prayed it wasn't an emergency. I had things to do, I told myself. Guilt ruined the day anyway.

You told me you'd taken a taxi to the shops. It had cost a fortune. You were still alive.

You have much better stories than this one, which is a shame because it is this story that will now define you. I prefer the story when your thirteen-year-old self went scrumping for apples and the police came. You were hiding up the tree. They'd never have known had your friend not fallen out and landed at their feet. Or, my favourite of all your stories: the one where you first held a tiny baby me in your arms and fell instantly in love.

You must be out, I thought, as I drove past your house today, on the way to the dentist. I didn't see your car. Then, I remembered.

That Year

Helen O'Sullivan

I have a terror of being killed by a tree. It happened to a woman near where we once lived. As I walk down the tree-lined avenue, the roar behind me is so loud I step onto the verge to avoid being hit by a car. Looking round, there is nothing but the wind driving up off the valley, threatening to blow me into the road.

I turn my back to it, just as I did to the approaching car the day one of my young twins danced giddily into the road. Thankfully, the car stopped before my human shield. Perhaps less than being a grand protector, I was just turning my back on danger. Is it natural to do so, thinking what you can't see won't hurt you? It reminds me of young children who cover their eyes to make themselves "invisible".

Now, as I take this January walk in 2020, I wonder if this is what we are doing when it comes to climate change? If we do not look at it – do not confront it and turn our backs – it will go away, and it cannot get us. If only.

It turns out that George Marshall has written a book about this: Don't Even Think About It – Why Our Brains are Wired to Ignore Climate Change. He explains how our need to fit into social groups, to seek enemies and to confirm our own biases, has politicised a set of ideas put forward by scientists who are meant to be concerned not with politics but seeking rational truth.

Climate change makes us uncomfortable because the enemy is us and confronting it means pointing the finger at ourselves. It means changing habits, values, beliefs and perceptions, and that is frightening, even before climate disaster strikes (as it already has). But in a real emergency, we are pushed back to the simple physics of life and our needs for food, water, warmth, and shelter. Differing beliefs and opinions seem trivial – a luxury. We are called on us to forget all the daily activities which confirm our social status and to see ourselves as we really are – vulnerable animals in a wild world. I suppose we can acknowledge this and protect ourselves, or we can just sit and wait to be eaten.

I begin the new year with a firm resolution: to cut down on family waste and save the planet by reducing our carbon footprint, even ever so slightly. To begin with, I will buy all the aspirational tools to make this possible. The irony of this is not lost on me. Zero waste has its own market. On the blustery walk, I muse about how much the expensive bamboo toothbrushes and floral beeswax wraps might shield me from the climate's storms.

Over the road, two golfers glance at the scene across the valley. They are not wearing rain jackets – just baseball caps. The wind forces rain into my face, and I feel like my eyelashes are being blown off, with the flesh on my face rippling like liquid. How will the golfers account for the whipping wind in the trajectory of their golf balls? I wonder if I should head indoors, but either direction is a long way now.

Further on, a fallen tree branch has collapsed a fence between the avenue and the hotel beside it. I glance up at the trees, wondering if my anxiety will do me any good. Would I see a falling branch in time and jump out of the way? In the right direction? Or would I jump into harm's way by mistake? Or deliberately, perhaps? Overwhelming danger can have its own magnetic pull. I remember sitting on top of the cliffs at Dun Aengus on Inishmore, feeling the hypnotising draw of the vast sea. I had no death wish at all and moved well back, but still it called to me. 'Come in!' it said. 'Be one with me!'

I keep my steady pace against the wind.

***

Two months later, I am wiping all the plastic food packaging down with washing-up liquid on its arrival in the house. It takes a full forty minutes. I feel like a madwoman, but better safe than sorry. So much for zero waste. Unpackaged food no longer appeals. But wiping the raw cabbage with detergent was taking things a bit too far!

It is the fifth of March, 2020, and Covid-19 is spreading rapidly around the world, disrupting air travel, economies, and healthcare systems. It highlights our interconnection and our vulnerability. It also reveals the potential for immediate global action. Pollution over China has rapidly decreased. Nitrogen dioxide from motor vehicles, power plants, and industrial facilities has virtually disappeared over Wuhan where the breakout began. Governments have stopped planes, trains, and subways, and limited other vehicles. In the fight against climate change, the virus seems to be a silver lining.

My father-in-law mentions that someone in his town gets business supplies from Wuhan. A friend knows a café owner in town who fears bankruptcy now that Google employees are working from home. Schools have been closed in Italy. People must decide if their travel is necessary. Twenty-five thousand publishers, authors, and agents can no longer attend the London Book Fair. We are attuned only to those activities which are truly essential to survival in a way that no end of cajoling about climate change can achieve. As George Marshall makes so clear in his book, the fear of death from climate change is too remote. However, fear of death from this coronavirus is immediate – the consequences sudden.

I am exhausted. It is partly all the nervous energy of waiting and wondering if the government will act – tell us to stop, to stay home and not bring our children to school.

Strangely, in the days before lockdown, I had been out and met more people than I have in years. I celebrated a big birthday with my family in London and then in Dublin at the end of February, went to an alumni dinner, then met friends from my old mother-and-baby group. The anxiety was more and more palpable at each event. The awareness really started after London. We heard that someone travelled through Dublin airport a few days before us and brought the virus with them. We reassured ourselves that we had used the nappy-changing toilets at the airports, herding all three children inside and safely locking the door. The carrier was less likely to have been in those.

The next event was the dinner with friends and family in Dublin. One friend is a respiratory consultant in Beaumont. It felt reassuring, though anxiety still seemed a little over-the-top. As in everyday life, we were still suspicious of possible governmental "hype".

But how it is being dealt with does not seem to be so much mired in party politics as in expertise; the authoritative voices are scientists and medics. We have been launched into an unelected technocracy. Doctors and psychologists are all over the media telling us how to behave for our survival. On Primetime, a professor of biomedics humbly tells the Tánaiste that measures really need to be stepped up a gear. The Tánaiste stumbles over his words. Power has shifted.

We must willingly give up our rights to roam freely in order to contain the threat. To prevent the virus spreading, we must stop shaking hands and hugging each other, communicate via technology rather than face-to-face, work from home or not at all, and spend more time with our children – homeschooling. It is immediate and radical.

Greetings are the first noticeable change. By the time of the alumni dinner on March 7th, we are no longer shaking hands. Or at least, I automatically shake hands with two people on our table before my husband calls me out on it. I apologise immediately. I wonder if I should offer them hand sanitizer. But then I would look like I was infected! Awkward. We carry on as if nothing happened. At the end of the dinner, I move to another table where two of our friends are seated. One of them complains that the woman he was sitting next to was spitting at him as she talked.

A few minutes later, the same woman returns to the table, chats with us, coughs into her hand, and then, later, proffers the same hand to say goodbye. Unaccustomed to refusing a handshake, I find myself shaking hands, as does my friend beside me. The woman's husband waves her hand away and says gruffly, "No hand-shaking!"

"Oh, sorry!" And she is gone.

I think about how we were all raised to cough into our hands. You might as well just cough into someone's face. Later on, that is what some protesters will do to the gardaí.

I have been so occupied raising young children for the last seven years, that these social events are a huge breath of fresh air. The day before the school closures are announced, I feel a little run down. It is a familiar feeling, as if there is a virus lurking in my body that resurfaces when I am embattled by over-exertion – a slight sore throat, feeling a bit hot and cold, a snuffly nose. No fever. No cough. Not even really a cold. In another life, I would dismiss these symptoms and say they were a poor excuse for quitting on life, and unlikely to affect anyone else. But now I am not so sure. Again, not wanting to be overly nervous, I keep up my social appointments. I meet a friend for coffee. We remember not to hug when we arrive, but on parting we do so habitually.

At the mother-and-baby-group dinner, things are even more awkward, as no one has met for a long time. We narrowly avoid hugging, and end up patting each other on the shoulder instead. Everyone talks all evening of the virus and possible school closures, and wonders how to navigate going to the toilet, including how to open the door latch after washing your hands. Another mum says she opened it with a tissue. So many tricks to learn! The mother is a pathologist in Vincent's Hospital and wonders if she will be needed for virus testing. Anxiety is mounting.

The chilli in the dinner sets my nose running, and I have to blow it a lot. I feel the need to keep reapplying hand sanitizer. A woman on another table looks at me as she dines with her older mother. It's definitely time to retreat from the world.

Next morning, my three-year-old boy has climbed into bed next to me, sniffing and coughing. It is my turn to bring the children to school but I decide against it. Time to batten down the hatches.

The actual school closure the following day still takes us by surprise. My husband is at work and can only get to the supermarket at lunchtime. This is after the announcement. The queues run from the till to the next transverse aisle. There are no trolleys, so he waylays someone in the car park and gives them the coin before they put their trolley back. He stocks up on porridge. We can survive on that if there is nothing else!

I am relieved that something has finally been done. England has not been so restrictive. Even Cheltenham Festival is still going on, with hand sanitizers. My father has a hospital appointment for a blood perfusion test to check his arteries. It is not essential right now, but along he goes. He manages to knock out his canula reaching for a book, spraying radioactive blood all over the waiting room, which nurses hurry to mop up. His story brings a bit of light relief from the other goings on, but I worry about him visiting a hospital at all.

At first, the lockdown distracts me from my new year's resolution, but then with all the time at home, the opportunities for reducing waste by "growing your own" abound. A good few decades into my life on this planet, I am discovering something fundamental for the first time: the delight of seeds and plant growth! We sprout carrot tops, beans, and stick apple pips in soil. I have cabbage scraps sitting in water, and I lift one out to discover roots shooting out the bottom.

"Look at this!" I cry, foostering about to find more.

I am too slow, and my seven-year-old, in a new world-weary tone, stops me before he has seen it. "Yes, something is growing on the bottom." He pads away, tired of my constant joyous cries. Something else has grown. So what? Things grow. But I find it endlessly magical.

With not much else to do, we (or I) get a bit carried away. There are enticing videos online showing people whipping seeds out of all manner of fruits and vegetables, and getting things to shoot out of water until, kaboom, you have a bunch of bananas on your very own banana tree. The footage has been sped up. And who knows if it is their own tree? Anyway, we go and slice a banana lengthwise and ferret out sections with seeds to plop in some soil. On the phone, my seven-year-old excitedly tells his grandma that he will be growing bananas. She thankfully tempers his glee by explaining that they need tropical conditions. But who knows? Maybe it will succeed! My imagination works overtime. I picture growing a little sapling in the greenhouse, then bringing it into the house to tower over us, bananas ripening in our living room, worthy rivals to whatever spectacle is on television.

It seems in lockdown I may be better at going bananas than growing them, but all the seed sowing keeps the children educated and entertained, and helps me keep my new year's resolution, I think

On the fourth of April, Fintan O'Toole writes in the Irish Times about the effect of this coronavirus on the environment: *For us human beings, it is devastating, emotionally, socially, and economically. But for the planet, it is a holiday from our relentless foulness.*

Mobilized by the immediate threat of death, he says we have inadvertently made huge strides in adopting a way of life that serves the planet. There are blue skies over London. The waters of Venice run clear. Carbon monoxide in New York has dropped by fifty per cent. But for O'Toole, the whole notion of "saving the planet" is misguided, because we are the ones who need saving by protecting the host we "infect". In O'Toole's imagery, we are the planet's virus.

So, really, I ought to be as afraid of being a tree-killer as I am of trees killing me. In precarious times, it seems best to support our arboreal friends. Sowing seeds is a hopeful activity.

"Hey, children! Who wants to grow an oak tree?"

False Memories

Rory Dwayne

I remember,
Small bumps growing bigger.
Wet eyes, red blood.
Time passes, scars heal,
Shoulders you cried on,
Become no-man's-land.
I remember,
Oaths placed before God.
Not in matrimony.
Screaming at clouds,
Drifting away in the flood of time.
Sweet flavours,
Drunken glimpses,
Of who you were yesterday.
I remember,
Times when,
Happiness won.

I feel,
Times when,
Sadness felt real.
Your kiss,

On other lips,
Smashed jewellery,
Oh, sleepless nights.
I remember,
Yesterday,
But tomorrow,
Who will remember me?

The Stations

Mary Heern White

Also published in Ireland's Own, April Spring Special, dated April 1st 2025.

After Sunday Mass ended, Madge Heeran leaped from her seat like a young foal released into the fields for the first time. She rode her bicycle back home – only four miles away – with the determination of a racehorse at the Grand National. Her tummy fluttered as she threw her bike against the hawthorn hedge by the porch before bursting through their farmhouse door.

"Madge, what's the matter?" her husband Francie exclaimed, almost choking on his boiled egg. "Your face is as red as a ripe strawberry."

"Father McCabe chose us for the Station Mass this spring," she blurted out.

"Is that all? I thought you were being chased by a bull with how fast you rode down that lane."

"Francie, how will we afford to paint and make all the necessary improvements to spruce up the place for spring?"

"But did Father say we had to do all that?" Francie asked.

"You know he didn't, but it's expected," Madge replied, her tone firm.

Despite their tight budget and seven mouths to feed, Madge understood that once announced during Sunday Mass at St. Mary's

Church in Foxfield, there was no turning back from hosting the Station Mass. This centuries-old Catholic tradition, originating from Ireland's Penal Laws but preserved by Father McCabe's forty-year leadership in the parish, automatically invited all neighbours to participate. Yet, even with her tight budget, no one would dare look down on Madge Heeran or her family.

One early Saturday morning, braving harsh weather conditions, Madge cycled to Mohill in search of paints, Jeyes Fluid, and distemper for their outhouses, and struggled to cover the cost. She returned from Mass in a foul mood and urged everyone, including her quiet husband Francie, to rise and start preparing for the spring clean.

Ever since the paintbrushes were purchased, chaos reigned in the Heeran household for weeks. Each family member received specific tasks, which were meticulously inspected upon completion. The atmosphere was akin to a military operation, with no room for error tolerated. This rural religious tradition, where parishioners took turns hosting the Station Mass, demanded extensive spring cleaning and redecorating. Father McCabe viewed it as a unifying event for the community, culminating in a house blessing. However, not all parishioners shared his enthusiasm; some households declined their turn, citing their home's poor condition as a reason to opt out of participating. Consequently, Father McCabe refrained from personally asking individuals to host the Station Mass after realising how easily they could evade the responsibility with various excuses. Instead, he adopted a new approach of announcing the selected host during Mass, leaving no room for refusal.

Mary Teresa was assigned the painstaking task of washing every piece of china with lifelike forget-me-nots painted on them. She handled each delicate item with utmost care, mindful of preserving these heirlooms passed down through three generations. Seamus was tasked with arranging for the local chimney sweep to prevent any fire hazards on the day of the Station Mass. Regrettably, this arrangement took an unfortunate turn when the absent-minded sweep forgot to protect the furniture in the parlour with dust sheets. Madge's reaction was swift and fierce as she berated him and demanded his immediate departure along with his tools.

Francie hired a handyman to paint the hall but found himself constantly underfoot as Madge insisted she could have completed the task in half the time. Meanwhile, Liam faced challenges stacking logs for the fires he was commissioned to set up; his improper technique resulted in excessive smoke and smouldering flames. He had to remove all logs, chop them into smaller pieces using a hatchet, and rearrange them with great care before achieving a satisfactory blaze.

Sean and Tony had almost completed whitewashing the exterior walls of the house without incident, until Madge's discerning eye caught sight of missed spots and splattered windows. Her disapproval was evident as she promptly dispatched them on their bicycles to Ballinamore with strict instructions to return only with turpentine in hand. Just when it seemed peace was restored, a debate erupted over who would accompany the priest for a meal at the dining table post-Mass.

Tensions rose as poor Francie, attempting to please Madge, suggested various neighbours for stimulating conversation to impress Father McCabe. However, none met Madge's standards.

"Surely Ned Muldoon is perfect for engaging Father McCabe," Francie proposed with confidence, citing Ned's alleged encounter with the Blarney stone. "Between Ned and I, we'll keep Father McCabe entertained with our banter."

Madge scoffed at this notion. "Neither of you know a thing about religion... or much else for that matter."

Undeterred, Francie defended himself: "Religion? If that's what he fancies discussing, Father McCabe surely surpasses us all with his

Maynooth background. And what about the tradition of him dining alone in the parlour while we wait outside?"

Madge, on her knees scrubbing the flagstones, dismissed his musings as outdated rituals. "You should be painting the haggard gate instead."

Francie attempted to redirect attention by suggesting the curate could dine with Father McCabe. This sparked confusion among the group as they debated the existence of a curate in their area.

"I heard rumours of a curate joining the priest," Francie interjected, his nervousness clear in his attempt to diffuse Madge's mounting frustration. "They're grooming them to continue traditions once the older priests retire. The curate supposedly conducts confessions in the parlour while Mass is held in the kitchen... balancing communion duties with keeping an eye on dinner preparations."

Filled with seething rage at Francie's nonchalant attitude towards the urgent matter, Madge leapt up in a frenzy, sending the half-filled bucket of water crashing to the floor, splashing Jeyes Fluid all over the place.

"She'll be the death of us all!" Francie's panicked cry echoed as he hurried out of the kitchen, determined not to interfere with Madge until after the Station Mass had concluded.

Both Madge and Francie were gripped with anxiety over the financial strain looming over their household. Managing a family of seven on meagre earnings from their modest farm was a constant struggle. The impending burden of paying dues to the priest on the day of the Station Mass weighed heavily on Madge. Not only did the priest collect these contributions, but he also publicly disclosed each parishioner's donation in the following weeks.

The tradition of paying dues dated back to Penal times when parishioners were expected to provide fodder for the priests' horses. Madge found this practice archaic and unnecessary, fuelling her resentment towards it. When Father McCabe made an unexpected visit one morning to discuss preparations for the Station Mass, she couldn't contain her frustration.

"So, Madge and Francis, I see you're busy getting ready for the Station Mass," Father McCabe remarked with some cheer.

"We had little choice," Madge retorted, her tone sharp.

"You always have a choice, Madge. There's no need for extravagant displays to have a Mass said and receive blessings."

"We can't afford to stand out negatively now, can we, Father?"

"That seems to be a trend lately – neighbours competing to impress others instead of focusing on blessings and community unity."

Amidst the chaos of event preparations, Father McCabe's remark about Madge's knowledge of her Catholic faith added to her already frayed nerves. Feeling a surge of anger rising within her, she nudged Francie under the table for support. However, he remained composed, unmoving as the chimes of the tall grandfather clock in the corner echoed through the tense silence.

"Perhaps this year there won't be a need for collecting dues, given the focus on religion and community," Madge suggested, eager to challenge the priest. Francie shot her a warning look, silently urging her to refrain from further provocation while he patiently waited for the uncomfortable moment to pass.

"Just like a horse needs fodder, a car requires petrol to keep running," Father McCabe responded, his voice calm.

"We are in more prosperous times now, Father," Madge retorted. "I doubt such measures are necessary."

"Times are still tough, Madge."

"I am well aware," she conceded. "But could you kindly reconsider publicly announcing people's dues from the altar? It only serves to shame struggling families."

"You raise a valid point, Madge," he acknowledged. "I have always felt uneasy seeing parishioners squirm at such announcements."

"Good," she said. "Let's put an end to that then." With that decisive statement, she shot up, signalling for Francis to escort the priest out.

Her family erupted with joy upon learning that the humiliating tradition of announcing family names and dues collected at the Station Mass would finally cease.

On a beautiful spring morning, the Heeran family rose at dawn. Mary Teresa selected pink camellias from the garden and arranged them in two large vases positioned at either end of the kitchen table, enhancing the elegance of the white embroidered tablecloth. Madge placed a delicate set of cruets containing water and wine, accompanied by a finger bowl that also served as a manuterge, evoking an altar-like atmosphere in the room. Homemade fruit cakes filled biscuit tins on the sideboard, while foil-wrapped rhubarb tarts and a substantial portion of ham, large enough to feed the entire parish, were proudly displayed alongside garnished tomatoes and lettuce. A decanter, filled to the brim with brandy, was laid out for when the priest departed, adding a touch of luxury to the setting.

The kitchen and parlour were illuminated by two crackling fires, enveloping the house in a comforting warmth that beckoned neighbours to gather before the priest's arrival. Madge's family stood in their best attire, leaving only standing room available as they awaited the priest's entrance. The rooms and hallway quickly filled with guests, some even lingering halfway in and out of the house for fear of missing any part of the event.

Father McCabe and his curate – referred to by locals as a special envoy from Mohill – arrived punctually. Without delay, the curate was led to the parlour to begin confessions, while Father McCabe blessed a bucket of water at the doorstep before making his way through the crowded house. Shortly after, empty bottles were dipped into the newly blessed holy water to be taken home for sprinkling on doors and windows as protection against lightning strikes throughout the year.

It soon became evident that there were few sinners in this townland as penitents swiftly exited confession feeling relieved and renewed, ready to partake in Holy Communion. With his stole draped around his neck over his soutane, Father McCabe absolved each soul graciously before proceeding with Mass. Seamus was handed the altar bell while Liam took charge of serving Paten as everyone scrambled to find space to kneel.

After Mass concluded, Ned Muldoon hurried off to secure his place at the table for engaging conversation with Father McCabe out of concern for retaining his elective position. Once Father McCabe and his curate departed from sight, laughter filled the air, soon followed by lively songs played on violins and accompanied by rhythmic foot tapping. Appetites were whetted by Madge's food-laden platters making their rounds among parishioners, who joined in the merriment with drinks in hand; their souls cleansed through this enduring ritual of Station Mass.

Fragments Of My Mother

T.O. Munro

A sketch of my mother sat in my study for twenty years. I used to think how well she had posed – distracted by a toy – while the artist worked. Later, we found a black and white photo suggesting he had crafted the picture from a studio photograph. I wondered why my grandmother chose the more sombre, reflective pose to be artistically preserved. I wonder what the toy's name was.

Short Sight

Mum and Dad met at carefree Cambridge University as the 50s gave way to the 60s – he two years the elder, hardened by national service. A quarter of a century later, I was invited to dinner by a couple who had been their friends and contemporaries. They told the story of my parents' first date, waiting for each other on opposite sides of Trinity Street, too shortsighted without their glasses to recognise each other. The couple – witnessing this – had taken pity and brought them together. Without that charity, where would I be?

My First Hangover

I would have been five or six, confident I was of an age to discover why grown-ups made such a fuss over alcohol, and also of a height to circulate unnoticed at my parents' Christmas party, draining every glass within reach; low tables were fashionable in the 1960s. I remember acting a drunkenness I did not feel, no wiser about the lure of drink. Once nausea properly set in, I threw up over my sister's advent calendar. Joanna was furious. Why couldn't I have thrown up on my own calendar? My mother ministered to me with an unexpected coldness – I mean, I was sick. When you were sick, you got hugs and cuddles.

Mum the Hun

The family called me "Math" until dad discovered "Decline and Fall", a map and cardboard counter wargame he hoped might replace Monopoly as the family game of choice. We played it just once. Dad was the Romans because they had complicated special-economics rules. Joanna was the Vandals. I was the Goths.

My mother chose the Huns because they had least to do in the game. She sat smoking at the Eastern edge of the board while dad tried to manage us into enjoying it.

Though we never played it again, the moniker "Mum the Hun" helped me to slide neatly from "Math the Goth" to "Moth the Goth". The nickname stuck – I didn't become Matthew again until Dad remarried.

Breakdown

Memory comes in little gossamer threads. You hesitate to pull at them too hard for fear they will disintegrate or worse, that – by focusing too intently – you might manufacture a false narrative to frame and support them.

I remember my mother asking how I would feel about a baby brother or sister. I would have been eleven and I remember being quite keen on the idea, though the conversation was little more than a passing remark.

Later my parents were sitting on their bed. He had his arm around her. she was sad. Something had been discussed. Something had been agreed – the baby brother or sister was gone.

Mum became more fragile after that. Grandparent visits became more frequent. Granny Moo, getting out of a car fresh from a drive from Devon to London, assuring Mum: "It'll be all right, Moolet, I'm here." And Mum distraught and dismissive: "It'll never be all right." And me witnessing this from my bike and riding off in frustration, desperate to get away from the suffocating stench of depression. When I returned two hours later, they were out looking for me. They'd even called the police.

The fight on the stairs between Mum and Dad put me in a paralysis of misery. Joanna had the presence of mind to get help from the neighbours.

I remember visiting Mum when she was an inpatient at the Maudsley hospital, and crying because she wanted to come home and she wasn't allowed, and I'd never felt so helplessly sad before.

And Mum arguing in the kitchen at the Maudsley, insisting it was me and her against Dad and Joanna, lifting me up to sit on the worktop so we could be as tall as them, because that was what counted.

A slow recovery. Dad took us all on a rainswept family holiday on the Norfolk broads in a cabin cruiser named Halcyon III – a week of anything but Halcyon days. The diner was designed to be collapsed each night into the double bed for Mum and Dad but, once collapsed, it wasn't reconstituted as a table until the end of the holiday. Mum spent the days sitting in the bed, wig all askew, smoking.

Writing

I monopolised Mum's old typewriter in my early teens – spending each summer holiday bashing out another pseudo-Hornblower naval novel. Over the long weeks of August, my biorhythms would creep inexorably nocturnal, until birdsong accompanied me pulling the tenth page of my nightly routine free from the typewriter carriage. I'd sleep on the sofa until mid-afternoon, my dreams interrupted by Mum's exasperated cry: "Oh, Moth!"

I craved feedback, delivering the story in instalments to my parental beta readers. Dad, at least, was usually engaged enough to talk to me about the story – apart from the time he and Joanna sabotaged an early draft by inserting three whole paragraphs of my captains discussing the internal décor of their respective battleships.

Mum could not bring herself to be more than a proofreader. She corrected spelling and punctuation, but as far as plot and character were concerned, she followed the maxim: If you can't say anything nice, say nothing.

Tensing

Our Battersea Dogs' Home puppy was named for Edmund Hillary's sherpa companion – because of her determination to climb over the barrier of wine boxes Mum had assembled to confine her in the kitchen, though before long she was sleeping on Mum's bed.

Julia, a vet student friend of mine, was horrified at breakfast to find Tensing languidly sprawled on the kitchen table; she used a voice of command the dog had never heard before to send her scuttling down. The dog and Mum shared an unconditional love, each crediting the other with an absolute understanding of their needs.

Céad Míle Fáilte

Mum needed to orchestrate big celebrations, such as the themed engagement party for me and Ash – our small nuclear family padded out by the perennial device of inviting all my sister's in-laws. The shamrocks, the table decorations, and the homemade "Céad Míle Fáilte" banner, all part of Mum's determination to welcome Ash, and express her gratitude that someone would have shown an interest in me. Ash and I privately joked that – both nudging thirty – we were simply each other's last petrol station before the desert.

Faith

Mum was brought up a Catholic, Dad a Scottish Presbyterian. Their struggle to find a church that would marry them sparked Mum's deep disillusionment with the faith of her youth.

My sister had a secular wedding ceremony in Camberwell registry office. For a week beforehand, Mum and I went out every night, working under cover of darkness to collect binbags of litter from the registry office grounds; it was important the place should look its best for the wedding photos. My sister, future brother-in-law, and father spent that week holidaying in Scotland, escaping the pre-wedding tension between maternal and bridal expectations.

When Ash and I told Mum we were getting married in a catholic church, she said stiffly that it would have to be without her being there. We said, regretfully, so be it. She came anyway. Like the Korean war, Mum's dispute with Catholicism was never properly settled, the two sides grinding uneasily alongside each other – tectonic plates, prone to sudden shifts.

First Grandchild

Ellie-Jo was born early on Friday 7th May 1993. It was not an easy birth. Uncertainty over whether Ash's waters had gone meant she was induced two weeks early. A long night in maternity ensued: two attempts at an epidural; a cupboard full of cardboard kidney dishes used up for Ash to vomit in; a tottering tower of glass attached to her wrist, feeding a three-way combination of drugs through a needle that looked long enough to have reached her elbow; a midwife giving me a side-eyed comment "We have been reading the maternity books, haven't we?" when I tried to say I believed Ash was in the transition phase.

And in the midst of this, we were told that my mother had arrived and I exclaimed, "What the fuck is *she* doing here!", only to step outside the room and find Mum waiting at the door, laden with unsuitable supplies of drinks and sandwiches, pregnant with expectation for her first grandchild. She didn't stay. We both knew she'd heard me, but we never mentioned it.

Diagnosis

Mum embraced middle-aged spread almost fondly as she passed through her fifties, but then acute symptoms demanded an emergency admission to a private hospital in North London. With four children under ten, it was difficult for me and Ash to do any visiting, except as a collective. When we sat one-year-old Tess on Mum's lap in the hospital bed, I saw a sadness in her eyes as she let the baby play with her yellowed fingers – a knowledge that this grandchild would never know her well enough to remember.

I managed one evening visit to Mum by myself. She was resting but directed me to a drawer, to a letter from her consultant she wanted me to read. I knew the diagnosis already. Dad had told me this was terminal – a cancer the specialist was unused to seeing "presented so late". But we could not talk about it.

As I had approached my teens, I found a sex-education book she must have left on the coffee table for me to discover. I'd consumed it avidly, but its stylised pictures and constant references to "excitement" seemed as unenlightening as the incomprehensible jokes I was being told in school.

Thirty years later, death remained as unspoken as sex had been, a matter to be shared and understood only through someone else's written words. Perhaps the book was meant to trigger questions. Perhaps the letter was supposed to kickstart a discussion. Whatever the reason, I digested them both without comment.

Progression

Mum was discharged to a bed in the front room at home. She'd sit up, smoking away, cheerfully asserting there was nothing to be gained by giving up cigarettes now. Nobody dared to point out the explosive risk to the house, indeed the neighbourhood, with a naked flame so close to the oxygen canisters by her bed.

On what turned out to be the last weekend, Dad took a break from the continuous care duty so my pregnant sister and I had a couple of days alone with my mother.

She was a shrunken thing by then – the ironic affectation of a poorly worn wig at last abandoned – thin, sleeping on one living room sofa. I slept on the other sofa. Mum's pain seemed poorly managed, the cancer in her bones, but there was no way she would return to hospital. I found some athletics on the TV, and though her eyesight wasn't great, we sat and for a moment imagined ourselves back in 1980, the summer Coe and Ovett took turns at breaking records around Europe, Mum ruthlessly partisan for Coe, the pair of us united in a joy that set us apart from the rest of the family.

Dad and Joanna sent me away – a Sunday it must have been – back to Kent and my family. My phone woke us in the middle of the night, buzzing in the kitchen where I got to it too late. We answered it the second time it rang, Dad telling me to come – it was time.

The third call came when I was driving up the A2, near the crest of the hill before Bluewater, with Annie Lennox playing on the car CD. Dad told me Mum had died – thought I might want to turn back. I drove on.

Flowers

The world doesn't stop when someone dies. We still had a new-build house we were a fortnight away from moving into. Grief came not in waves but in needle-sharp triggers that pierced the shield of mundane normality and sucked me into a void: a brief word of condolence from Nick the builder, touching in the stranger's simple sincerity; ordering flowers when words so totally deserted me – as I tried to describe the four single roses we wanted from Mum's grand-children – that I had to dumbly pass the phone to Ash; seeing the coffin and how the undertakers had threaded those roses, one through each of its four handles.

I didn't cry, as I feared I might, when I spoke at the crematorium service, nor did Ellie-Jo, reading her own tribute. Niamh gurned her eyes out from the moment she saw the coffin, distraught until at last she could park herself by the canape table back at the house for the reception. Maisie played happily enough with Joanna's son William, both too young to be hollowed out by grief.

Ashes

Dad bought a spot in the cemetery for Mum's ashes, but the three of us agreed they would be better scattered in Dulwich Park where she and Tensing had enjoyed leisurely walks. However, we were unsure what protocols might be involved and feared an embarrassing reprimand from a warden. So we decanted the ashes into different containers – one of them a wine bottle – and spent a dimly lit morning skulking in different directions around the park, shaking the ashes out like a trio of Allied prisoners of war disposing of dirt from the latest escape tunnel.

We buried an urn filled with brown sugar and a dog's collar in the cemetery plot. The plaque read *"In a better place"*.

Mum would have appreciated all of that.

A Lovely Day in the Neighbourhood

Eighteen years later, sitting with Ash in Dundonald Omniplex, Tom Hanks as Mr Rogers is quizzing Lloyd the journalist about the soft toy he *must* have had as a child, until Lloyd confesses it was a rabbit, called Old Rabbit.

Children are so literal in their toy names. I bought Woolly Dog for sixpence at a jumble sale, a knitted brown sausage dog. He once stood proud, well-stuffed, with orange beady eyes, but use made his legs loose, and a tight fist in search of comfort gradually squeezed the stuffing from his neck, turning his head all floppy. He disappeared when I was about ten, but resurfaced among my mother's effects, squirrelled away as memorabilia, along with my favourite yellow T-shirt from Brazil.

She must have put those things aside for me.

A Lasting Impression

Ethel Corduff

A human penguin gently
Took my hand from Mammy's.
Settling me between márla* and sand
In a small wooden box,
I was torn between the two delights.
I peeped at Mammy.
She smiled encouragingly.
I stuck a red plastic spade in the sand
And diligently filled the green bucket.
Sister Baptista waved to Mammy to go.
I got up to go after her,
But she was too quick.
Soon, I was totally absorbed in play.

Sister Baptista was wonderful,
Gentle with the little ones.
I remember how happy
I was in that classroom then.
No one could match her love and attitude.
After that auspicious year, school was a painful chore,
All the adult years, I thought of her with affection.

In middle age, I returned to the convent to see her.
In her eighties, she looked a little more lined,
But little else, not a wisp of hair, was to be seen.
Sister Baptista welcomed me, but barely remembered me.

She talked about how my mother helped the poor.
My sister, she recalled, glowingly.
She told a cameo tale about my brother.
The torch, I had carried in my head, extinguished a little.
Sometimes it is better to have only the memory.

Get to Know the Author

Róisín Coyne published her first novel, 'Mystery Behind the Bookshelf,' in 2023, at the age of eighteen. In 2024, 'The Fifth Element,' was released, and she is currently working on her third book. Róisín is autistic and has epilepsy, and believes a diagnosis doesn't mean the world cannot be your oyster.

Gráinne Soldic is a published writer of two novellas, 'Breathe and Bloom,' and 'Comings and Goings,' as well as blogs, poetry and short stories.

Kay Forristal lives in Waterford. Kay is the author of a novella called 'Dancing on the Edge,' and four poetry books, 'Praise the Living,' 'Yet Another Day,' 'The Turning Tide,' 'Goat's Apples.' She is currently working on her fifth book of poetry and prose.

Martin Hand has published two independent novels, 'The Green Platoon,' (2020), and 'The Devil's Countdown,' (2023). 'Vanessa's Ghost,' is due in 2026. The author lives and works in Dublin. Martin likes to explore themes concerning Christian mysticism.

Emma Davis is the proud author of two children's books, Three Mucky Pups and Pups, Pancakes and Pandemonium. Her poetry has been exhibited by Cork City Council for Poetry in the Park in 2022, and with Writeminds Poetry and Wellness. Emma edited our poetry for this collection. She is currently working on her debut poetry collection. fairyfortpublicati.wixsite.com/mysite

Leigh Kenny lives by the Irish Sea with the love of her life, two wonderful boys, a black Labrador, and a three-legged cat, who hates people. Her love of all things horror is usually evident in the stories she writes (and reads). You can find out more about Leigh's work and any upcoming releases on her social media pages.

DC Speura more usually just DC, is an avid author, playwright, and podcaster. "I have a deep passion for writing. I find myself addicted to exploring and discovering the many myths and legends of ancient Ireland." His podcasts and social media on Irish folklore have gained thousands of followers worldwide.

Fiona Gill is multidisciplinary artist encompassing music, writing, and illustration. She has a profound connection to music, viewing it as a sanctuary for expression and emotional exploration. As an author and illustrator, she is driven by an enduring love for all artistic forms. In 2024, Fiona released her first Children's Picture Book "I'll Be There".

Betty O Mahony received an M.A. in creative writing at University College, Cork in 2020. Betty received her B.A. from UCC in 2019, after taking early retirement in March, 2016, from the Central Statistics Office. She studied English and History of Art. She loves to write poetry and prose, sometimes combining both disciplines, and is delighted with having free time for writing since her retirement.

John Joe McGinley is passionate about history and family. He lives in Gweedore, County Donegal, along the Wild Atlantic Way. He is a writer, podcaster, blogger, radio host, and campaigner for autism awareness. He also writes for Ireland's Own, Irish Voice, the Irish Central, and on Irish story websites, and American history.

David Bowmore is a Michelin star chef, an award-winning teacher, a terrible gardener, and sometimes embellishes the truth. His stories have appeared in more than seventy-five publications, and he has released two books set in the mysterious town of Deben Market. David currently dwells in Yorkshire with his wonderful wife, Jai.

Eoin Brady is a writer from Drogheda. He is best known for 'Weep,' an ongoing post-apocalyptic series set in Ireland.

Catherine Kullmann is the author of eight novels that are set in the extended regency period, against a background of the offstage, Napoleonic wars. They consider, in particular, the situation of women trapped in a patriarchal society. Born and brought up in Dublin, she now lives there again. http://www.catherinekullmann.com/

Anne McDonald is an award-winning poet, whose first collection of poetry, 'Crow's Books,' was published in 2020, and her second collection, 'Clothes-peg in my Pocket,' will be published in 2025. Her writing has also been featured on collaborations with musicians and animators, and reviewed and broadcast on RTE Radio.

Eamon Ó Cléirigh, from Dublin, is living in Sligo since 2003. He writes fiction and poetry, and is currently developing a Dublin-based thriller, with another two in the proverbial drawer. All three will find their way out to the wider world...soon! He is a freelance online editor.

Mary Minnock is a French translator and editor, but her first love has always been writing fiction. After years of scribbling away, she finally decided to self-publish her first novel, 'Homesick,' in 2023, and her second,' Love Lost,' in November 2024. She is currently working on her third novel.

Eileen Moynihan is the SCBWI Ireland-Midlands co-ordinator and a member of Longford Writers Group. She has self-published 7 children's books and a collection of poetry. She has had short stories and poems in many anthologies. Eileen was born in England but has lived in Ireland since 1978.

Bernadette O'Reilly has been published in various journals and blogs. She has read on radio, and at open mics in Dublin City. She has self-published a book of poems called 'Gentle Touch.'

Mary M. Trant is a native of Co. Kerry, Ireland. Inspired by her creative ancestors, her hand-knitted creations have found homes across the globe. Recently, her debut book 'Life Between the Mountains and the Sea, A Memoir of an Irish Childhood,' offers a captivating insight into some marvellous childhood adventures.

Alex Secam's stories are soaked in bad luck and dark traumas. He explores an Ireland of dystopian horror. Sure, you have the Emerald Isle, the Land of Saints and Scholars, a warm pub with a turf fire. But the cosy island is also a land of surreal violence, corrupted societies, and ancient horrors. He writes from Cork, in Ireland.

Joanne Ryan Curran lives in Co. Louth, and in her spare time writes stories full of magic. She was selected for a publishing mentorship with An Táin Arts Centre. 'The Cards That Changed My Life,' her debut novel was published in 2024. She is now working on her second novel.

Originally from Offaly and now living in Cork, **Yvonne Brewer** released her second poetry collection, 'The Woman who Talked to Stones,' in 2023. She had a poem selected for Poetry in The Park, Cork, in 2021, and has been a participant for several years in 'Eat the Storms' poetry podcast for Poetry Day, Ireland.

Val Robus is an award-winning photographer, social media manager and blogger. She is enthusiastic about Sligo, Ireland, and interested in travel, adventures, food, and exploring. Val writes regularly on her blog magnumlady.com, and she released a book alongside poet, Louise G Cole, in November 2024.

Kathryn M. Crowley writes poetry and prose. She also contributes nonfiction to various publications. Her journalism is complimented by a lifelong arts practice. Kathryn's poetry has been widely published; however, she prefers to share it at live events. Read more at: https://kathryncrowley.eu/blog

After retiring, **Eamon O' Leary** started writing short stories and stopped hacking up the golf course. Better with pen than putter, his eclectic mix of stories has been widely published. He is a regular on A Word in Edgeways, on RTE Radio.' I'm a Big Boy Now,' his humorous collection of childhood memories, was published in Oct'24.

A Pushcart prize nominee, and author of two poetry collections to date, **Niall O'Connor** lives near the centre of Ireland, on the tribal lands of his ancestors, Firceall. Memories are seen as a glance into parallel universes, all coexisting at the same time, as opposed to the view that they are dead, and safely consigned to the past.

Tom Moloney has published three poetry collections, (2009, 2015, 2024), two novels, (2015, 2024), one short story collection, (2021). He has read his poetry on RTE 1, local radio, community film, online, and at open mic sessions in the Mid-West. He is a member of two writers' groups.

Robert McDermott lives and works in Dublin. He has written a novel, 'Jonestown', and a short story collection, 'The Occulting Light,' both published by Riversong Press.

Camilla Galbiati is originally from Italy, but she has been living in county Sligo since 2012. She has always loved writing. In 2024, she published her debut novel, 'Beatrice's Fate.' It is a historical fiction novel, full of romance and drama, set in 17th century Italy.

Orla McConnon Bakeberg is an Irish photographer, poet and artist from Mayo, who self-published her debut book, 'Life Threads,' in 2023. A creative entrepreneur, she captures nature's beauty through photography and poetry. She hosts creative writing courses, which inspire others to explore their artistic passions, and document life's vibrant moments.

Author of Fiction, with a number of books in the publishing process, **Mary Egan Campbell**'s poetry has been published in 'Whisperings,' in 2018, and 'Journeys,' in 2023. Both were published by Choice Publishing. She was long listed for the Fish Poetry prize in 2018, and shares poetry and blogs on social media.

Mary T Bradford is an Irish-published author of novels, novellas, and short story collections. Her work appears in newspapers and magazines too. Mary enjoys crocheting to unwind from stories that may be tumbling around in her mind. Visit her website: https://marytbradford.wordpress.com Her books are available on Amazon.

Denis Ahern is a dedicated personal development and wellness coach, specializing in energy-focused therapies. A single parent to a teenager, Denis balances family life with his passions for the gym, swimming, and writing. As the author of 'Breaking the Shackles,' he inspires others to overcome challenges and embrace personal growth.

Kerry Manning lives in the West of Ireland, and loves immersing herself in fictional stories, based on the Wild Atlantic Way. Her debut novel, 'Learning to Love Lucy,' will be released in 2025.

Theresa Hiney Tinggal was born in 1954, and raised in Dublin. At the age of 48, she discovered that she was not the biological child of her parents. She learned there were thousands like her, taken from single mothers in Ireland for decades, and illegally registered/adopted. Her poem is dedicated to all those mothers.

Carolann Copland has written three novels; 'Summer Triangle,' 'Scarred,' and 'Mosaic.' She has an MA in creative writing and facilitates both online and in person creative writing workshops. Carolann founded Carousel Writers before launching The Carousel Aware Prize for Independent Authors, in 2016, and is curator of Knocklyon Literary Festival.

Martin Daly is a retired Stone Mason and Financial Analyst (It's complicated...)He is a two-time winner of Cork City Folk Festival song writing competition. Short-listed: Fish Publishing Flash-Fiction Prize - 2023 Long-listed: Fish Publishing Short-Story Prize - 2024. Email address: andrew martindaly@gmail.com

Sandra Matthews is a Dublin poet. Her style is real and relatable. One poem may have you deep in thought, and the next have you laughing. In her books, you may find words about menopause, bereavement, farts, or any other subject life brings our way.

After a career spanning restaurant management, teaching, and retail, **Aislinn O'Neill** undertook a creative writing MA at Queen's University, Belfast, securing a distinction. Her work includes 'Confirmation' - a short story in the 2024 CAP prize-winning anthology, 'North Star.' She is currently working on her first novel, 'Unknown Pleasures.'

Claire O'Connor lives in West Cork. She published Over The Wall, in 2024. She has contributed to various anthologies since graduating an arts degree in 2009. In 2023, she and a friend co-founded Indie Authors Ireland. She enjoys writing shorts & poetry and published an ebook collection, V is for Vignettes & Verses. Claire hopes to publish her second collection in 2025 & the third novel in her trilogy in 2026.

Helen O'Sullivan is the author of the children's chapter book series, 'The Gollogans,' set in the woods of Dublin/Wicklow. She is a keen language learner and teacher, and a mother of three woodland explorers.

Rory C.J. Dwayne is an artist and writer living in the midlands of Ireland. He has over fifteen books, self-published, from horror anthologies, to children's picture books, and everything in between.

Mary Heeran White lives in Ennis. She holds an MA in creative writing. Her poetry is published in Creative Ireland, and Commemoration Ireland, (2023). She won first place at The Knocklyon Literary Festival, (2024).'Wild Atlantic Anthology: Characters Along Ireland's Majestic Coast (Vol. 1),' was shortlisted for the CAP Awards, (2024).

T.O. Munro started writing in his teens, and has three self-published fantasy novels. He has a PhD in Creative Writing, focusing on climate change fiction. He teaches an open-learning creative writing course at Queen's University, Belfast. He also writes articles and book reviews for the fantasy hive blog site https://fantasy-hive.co.uk

Ethel Corduff is a retired nurse from Tralee, Co. Kerry. She has a BSc (Hons) in Health and Irish Studies and has published articles, short stories and poems. In 2021, she published 'Ireland's Loss, Britain's Gain: Irish Nurses in Britain – Nightingale to Millennium,' and a memoir, in 2023, 'Blackberries and Crubeens.'

About Indie Authors Ireland

Indie Authors Ireland was set up as a facebook group in August 2023. Since then the group has gone from strength to strength. Last September we held our first event in Ballinasloe, with a great turnout and a yen for more! The group is a community for independent authors self publishing, or working with small press or hybrid services. We are a warm community of all types of writers and authors.

This anthology has been our biggest group project yet, and we are currently working on our September event for 2025!

A note about the use of AI: Our group, as a whole, is adamantly against the use of generative AI. No AI will be used in any of our publications.

If you are an indie author looking for a closed friendly community you can find us on FB via this link https://www.facebook.com/groups/irishindieauthors/

Printed in Great Britain
by Amazon

63069244R00139